THE MORMON MARSHAL

JACK R. STANLEY

WRIGHTRIDGE PRESS

ISBN: 978-1-947726-47-5
Wrightbrodge Press

Credits:
Cover by
Keith Diamond

TO GET TWO FREE E-NOVELS
BY
JACK R. STANLEY

MURDER IN MULESHOE

There's a killer in town. Do we hunt the S.O.B. down or throw him a parade?

GUNS ALONG THE RIO

Two fresh-off-the-ranch 17-year-olds join the Texas Rangers in 1858. What could possibly go wrong?

CLICK HERE

For my Family

CHAPTER 1

"I'm goin' t' kill you fer that! Get t' your feet, you son of a bitch!"

The scruffy gambler in the stained frock coat and bowler hat looked like he wasn't any better at a dining table with a spoon than he was with a deck of cards. He stood across the table from me while the other three players almost pissed themselves trying to get out of any line of fire. I sat back in my chair with my legs crossed.

"I didn't say you were cheatin'," I said. "I just think you're playin' with more cards than the rest of us."

"That's cheatin'!"

"I'll have t' take your word for it. You seem to know more about this than I do."

After a long day on the trail I had stopped in the only saloon in this one whore town for a drink and a friendly hand or two of cards. I know Mormon's ain't supposed t' drink Leapord Piss, but I wasn't one of the best Saints God ever made.

The whore was frumpy and leaning very hard toward the ugly side of plain as she was napping at the end of the bar. My guess was she did her best work in the dark with a partner who had the benefit of a good night's worth of whiskey. Tonight she wasn't doing any business and looked up at the noise where the three gents and I were playing the only game in town. Her name was Gert and she shot a quick glance over at the skinny barkeep who was watching the ruckus develop.

"Now, you goin' stand up and draw," the gambler said, "or sit there and wait for me to plug you?"

"B'fore you can pull your hogleg, you'll have to drop that card you palmed," I told him.

The expression on his face changed. He seemed to lose his color suddenly.

"That'll slow you down just enough," I said, "--- and you'll be dead 'fore you clear leather."

"Hell!" he almost shouted at me. "We should be about even 'cause you'll have to get to your feet to draw."

"Better look closer. I've already filled my hand," I said making two audible clicks with the hammer of my Schofield .44-40 revolver, "and I don't need to draw it."

"You goin'a shoot from your holster? Plannin' on blowin' your leg off while you're at it?" he smiled thinking he had me buffaloed.

"Nope. See how I have my leg crossed? And my knee raised?"

The bar was very quiet now.

"I'll give you the fact that the bullet is going to have to go through the table -- but it'll still smack you at about the third button of your vest -- right next to that gravy stain."

No one in the saloon moved. If it's clear that your life flashes before your eyes right before you die, I don't think the gambler liked the tintypes he was seeing. He blinked and swallowed hard; sweat popped out on his forehead as he caught his breath.

"Unbuckle your rig," I said once he started breathing again.

"It's tied down," he said after a moment having decided he liked living.

"Either your pistol hits the floor or you do. I hope your hammer's restin' on an empty cylinder or you just might shoot yourself if it lands wrong."

He didn't say anything but his left hand eased over and slipped the strap out of the buckle. His holster slipped down and his Army Colt dropped out and hit the planked floor where it flopped over and lay still. The tie down thong kept the rig dangling from his knee.

"Shuck the hideout up your left sleeve, too," I told him.

Slowly he used his right hand to slide an over and under two barreled .32 caliber Derringer down his left sleeve. It appeared in a scissor type of paraphernalia.

"Open it and drop the bullets on the table. Then you can put it in your coat pocket."

He followed instructions well.

When he was done, I got to my feet.

"Kick your pistol over to me."

He did and I picked it up never taking my eyes off of him or my hand off my pistol grip. Next I emptied five .45 caliber rounds onto the money pot in the center of the table. I tossed him back his pistol which he caught with both hands in the middle of his chest.

"Now the card," I told him.

By this point he had no choice. The six of diamonds landed face up as the other card players, a big-handed, wiry teamster, and a balding whiskey drummer watched with open mouths.

"He was cheatin'," the teamster growled.

"No wonder I was getting' beat s' bad," the whiskey drummer said.

"We ain't lettin' him out of here in one piece are we?" the farmer asked flexing his fingers into a fist. "He owes us."

I motioned to the gambler with my head to move toward the front door. He moved quickly his holster and gun belt dragging behind him.

"Your money's on the table. Which do you want -- it or him?" I asked keeping my eyes on the gambler as he reached the doors and pushed his way out into the night.

There was no doubt in the drummer's mind. He stepped over to the table and began counting. The teamster decided he had better keep his eyes on the money. The farmer joined them saying, "Seven dollars of that is mine."

The others claimed their share of the pot and the drummer looked over at me.

"What did you have in, mister?"

"Five bucks and six bits," I said still watching the door.

"There's twelve dollars and four bits left," the drummer announced after counting out my share.

"Twelve and a half bucks left," the teamster said.

"We're goin'a split that ain't we?" the drummer wanted to know.

"Weren't us that caught him," said the farmer. "All I want is what's mine. I knew better than to do this. I'm goin' home."

"Not, yet," I said holding out an arm and stopping the farmer. I turned to the skinny barkeep. "Did any of you hear anybody mount up and ride off?"

The barkeep shook his long face.

"Who wants to be the first one out that door?" I asked.

No one did.

"We can go out the back door," the drummer said.

"Where's your horse?" I asked the drummer.

"Tied up out -- front," he said realizing the stupidity of his suggestion.

"Everybody get away from this table," I said. "I don't think this is over, just yet."

CHAPTER 2

My name is Joshua Guymon and I've never thought of myself as a particularly religious much less a righteous man. And as for being Mormon -- well, Mama read us the Bible and The Book of Mormon from cover to cover while we were young. I go to church pretty much every week. But I do drink when I feel the need and I like a friendly game of cards. I even drink coffee now and again. Plus I was ready to kill that gambler if it had come to it.

Emma, my beautiful wife, sees to it that I take care of most of the reading and praying needed around our place. It's supposed to be my place. She's the one who takes care of the house and me. I expect I'm a lot more trouble than our little house.

I take care of our cattle and horses, the fences, tending the garden -- and Emma.

Papa and Mama joined the church in Nauvoo, Illinois before I was born. But three brothers and two sisters were already part of the family. The church had come from New York to Ohio and then to Illinois. There always seemed to be folks who didn't like or anyone who followed him.

To hear Mama tell it, Nauvoo was more of a swamp than good

land, but that's where the Prophet, Joseph Smith, was told to go. Then he and his brother Hyrum were murdered by a mob in Carthage.

The church stayed where it was for two more years til' our second prophet, Brigham Young, had a vision we needed to move on west. That's how we ended up in Deseret. That's our promise land, President Young told us. The United States has been chopping away at it to make the territories of Arizona, Idaho, and Wyoming. What's left is now called Utah Territory.

Bishop Douglas is the one who chose Papa and Mama along with other families to go East from Salt Lake with him across the line into Star Valley, south of Jackson Hole in Wyoming. Our mission was to create a new ward.

It was a time when the U.S. government was making it hard on us every way they could. Seemed our notions about plural marriage was what most folks seemed to hate the most about us. Papa never had a second wife or even wanted one as far as I knew. By then there were seven kids and our family and friends were about the only people we had much dealing with.

When I was seventeen, I took a job driving a stage from Jackson into Idaho Falls down to Salt Lake and back. That's where I met Emma.

She caught my eye as she boarded along with two drummers and the three women; Emma, her mother, and younger sister. Emma was just sixteen at the time and her sister was thirteen. One of the salesmen was a big, loud man with hardly any hair and blood shot eyes.

We were headed down to Salt Lake when the drummer started haranguing the whole stage about the fact that he was a Christian and the Mormon's weren't. When he found out Emma, her mother and sister were Mormons he began berating them.

About a half dozen miles out of the Falls I pulled up, climbed down, yanked open the door and pulled the drummer out by his collar. I threw him over my shoulder where he landed on his head and didn't move.

"You've killed him," the other drummer said. "He was drunk and didn't know what he was saying."

"He knew," I said. "And some people need killin'. It's the only way to teach'em manners." I looked at the women and said. "The Bible tells us it's not what goes in your mouth but what comes out of it that defiles you."

"He's moving," Emma said pointing to the man on the ground.

I turned and sure enough he rolled over groaning.

Stepping over to him I said, "You've about spent your ticket money with your mouth, mister."

"You can't leave him out here," the other drummer said.

"It wouldn't be just," Emma's mother said.

"Then he's riding up top with me," I said picking him up and hoisting him onto the roof of the coach. "That way if he says something he shouldn't, I can correct him without having to stop."

I closed the stage door and climbed back into the driver's seat. I looked back at the drummer rubbing his head and moaning.

"You best hang on, mister, cause if you fall off that's going to be your never mind."

I snapped the reins and we were off again.

Except for moans and groans the drummer up top was quiet. He had to pay attention to where we were going so he could hang on.

When we unloaded in Salt Lake, I introduced myself to Emma's mother, to Emma and her sister. Her mother invited me to have dinner with them in the hotel. They were to be met by her husband and Emma's father the next day.

I cleaned up and did eat with them although I have no idea what the food was. I couldn't take my eyes off of Emma and her soft red hair.

A year later Emma and I were married in St. George Temple, the first temple in Utah. I had built a house on the land I was clearing with the help of Papa and my brothers. It was to be where Emma and

I made our home. It was a good life and I never planned on going anywhere else. I did have an adventure when I was younger but now -- well now I didn't plan on going anywhere else. I wished now I had stuck to that notion a little better.

CHAPTER 3

"It'd be a good idea to get away from this table," I told the other players in the poker game. "And we ought t' dim the lights," I said to everyone in the saloon.

There were two posts evenly spaced away from the bar in the center of the room. They stood holding up the structure. I stepped over behind the nearest one. It didn't offer much in the way of cover cause I was a big target. I stood six foot two and weighted about two hundred and ten pounds -- or up to two twenty if I'd been home eatin' Emma's cookin' for a while.

After a few moments in which no one had anything t' say, the gambler kicked open the front doors and fired blindly toward the table where we'd been havin' our game. He didn't see me behind the post with my revolver in my hand, but I wasn't going to pull the trigger unless I had no choice.

But the barkeep cut loose with both barrels of the .10 gage he had laying cross the bar. The gambler was almost ripped in half from the double load of buckshot and was dead before his body flopped back in the dirt outside. The only thing he'd accomplished was punching a couple of holes in the wall behind the now empty table. I guess the proprietor took the disfiguring of his grungy establishment personally. He was within his rights. He reloaded both barrels of his scatter gun before he stepped around and went out to check the result of his work.

Everyone's ears rang from the gunplay inside the building. I stepped towards the door and noticed the barkeep cocked both hammers again before the stepped through the doors and stopped over the dead gambler.

"Figure you'll need t' shoot him again?" I asked.

"Any bastard who can stomach both barrels and ask for more is a man I aim to satisfy."

You can't argue with that kind of logic.

"Is there any law in this town?" I asked looking around the dark at the few other building in town.

"We never found the need for any," the barkeep said.

"Don't seem like we need any now," the farmer said joining us.

"He ain't goin'a need his game stake, now," the teamster said stepping around the pooling blood.

"What's it cost to get buried around here?" I asked.

"Seven bucks will cover Able, down t' the livery, buildin' a box and diggin' a hole," Gert said from the open door.

"That still leaves five and a half," the drummer said.

"I got expenses," the barkeep said.

"What expenses, Toby?" the farmer wanted to know.

"Holes in my wall. And how about Gert. She ain't worked in three days."

"She ain't had a bath in three weeks," the farmer said.

I leaned down and picked up the dead gambler's pistol. "Anybody know who he is?"

"Jest rode in this afternoon," skinny Toby said letting both hammers down easily. "From the South."

"Said his name was Phillips," Gert said. "Tom Phillips, from somewhere near St. Jo. 'Course he could be lyin.'"

I checked out the inside pockets of his coat and found another deck of cards.

"Why don't you see to his plantin'?" I said to the barkeep. I stepped over to his gelding and opened his saddle bags. All I found was a card trimming device I knew gamblers sometimes used and a shirt.

"He mention any family?" I ask Gert.

"I don't get paid for conversation," she said sarcastically. "He didn't seem to be interested in what I do best."

"Again, Gert," the farmer said, "that bath might be an investment worth takin'."

"Kiss my ass, Lynch," she shot back.

"If nobody objects, I'll take his pistols and his horse. I'm headed South and I'll check in the next town or two -- see if anybody there knows him or of any kin."

"Jest who the hell are you, fella?" Toby asked. "You're givin' a lot of directions to everybody."

"Name's Guymon. Joshua Guymon." I pulled open my vest and showed the tin star I had pinned to the inside. "I'm the sheriff out in Star Valley."

"That's Mormon territory ain't it?" the teamster asked.

"Yep," I said.

"You Mormon?"

"Yep," I repeated.

"That must make us all *Gentiles*," he said. "Don't know how I feel about that. In the Bible the Gentiles were the bad guys."

"Not bad — just none believers. The Pharisees were the bad guys."

"And why don't you have a beard?" the teamster asked. "Thought that was required."

"It's not a law — but most men do have one. I just can't get past the itchy stage of growing one."

"How come you didn't say nothing about bein' a sheriff b'fore," the whiskey drummer wanted to know.

"I came in lookin' for a drink and a few hands of cards. I'm off my range -- out of my jurisdiction."

"Ain't you back slidin' some, too? I mean, I hear Mormons don't take to drinkin' and gamblin'," Lynch the farmer said.

"We don't -- but sometimes I do. I never said I was a good Saint."

Changing the subject I said, "I'd like to write down what happened here and get everybody t' sign it if you would."

The group agreed and I started back inside.

The farmer asked me, "You married, Mormon?"

I nodded my head.

"How many wives?"

"One." I said. "You're married aren't you?" I asked Lynch.

"Yes. My Maude is one of the reason's I come to town," the farmer laughed.

"I'm of the opinion that it takes a special kind of married man to want more than one wife," I said.

"I think you're right there, mister," Lynch said.

The barkeep found some paper and a pencil.

"You ever seen Joseph Smith's golden tablets?" he asked.

"Nope," I said taking a seat at the first table I came to.

"I never saw the Garden of Edan, the Ten Commandments, nor the tomb where Jesus was buried, either. Doesn't mean I don't believe in them."

I began writing.

I thought this was over as soon as I finished noting where this gambler had come from and that I didn't know about if he had any kin -- but it wasn't.

CHAPTER 4

"Didn't know Star Valley had a sheriff," the burly Town Marshal of Alice Creek told me as he twirled one end of a mustache he seemed very proud of.

"For about a year now," I said showing him my badge inside my vest. "Bishop Douglas appointed me -- I expect 'cause nobody else would take the job."

"Joshua Guymon. I heard of you. They say you're hell on wheels with that Schofield you carry."

"I'd rather not have to use it."

"Did Tom Phillips want to give you a try?"

"We had a little conversation about it. But the barkeep in that no name town up the trail almost cut him in half with a .10 gage."

"He's been headed t' hell for long time. I'm not surprised how he got there."

"So, you did know him?"

"Whole town knew him. He made sure of that. He was even said to be friends with your brother, Micah."

"Did he have any family or kin you know of?"

"I don't even know if Tom Phillips was his real name. I do know he was a cheat and bully -- loud drunk. I could never prove it but I'll bet good money he knew his way into Hole In The Wall and had been involved with some of the goings on from that bunch."

"And you say he knew Micah?"

"They'd belly up to the bar together from time to time. There some other Mormons about. Didn't know Micah was one."

"Has Micah been into anything on the wrong side of the law?"

"Who's askin' -- the sheriff of Star Valley or his brother?"

"Both."

The marshal eyed me a minute before he said, "I've heard some things -- but nothin' I can prove. Not all you Saints are on the straight and narrow -- even as you see it."

"Guess I'm living proof of that. Say, Marshal, why don't you take Phillip's guns and his horse. If you can find someone who ought to have them ...." I didn't finish the remark as I gave him Phillip's gun belt and Colt along with the Derringer.

"If you're lookin' up your brother ---"

"That's the reason I'm down this way. Micah's married to Geneva, th' daughter of Stoops Cowen. They live out at Stoops ranch down on the Green River."

"Then you can take his mount with you. That's where this horse came from." Then after a pause he added, "Stoops is another Saint your prophet wouldn't be too proud of."

"Meaning?" I asked.

"Again, nothin' ever been proved — but Stoops has a reputation. You'll find out."

He gave me directions to the ranch.

Being down in the southwest corner of the Wyoming Territory, I took a few miles of the Oregon Trail to the river and found the Cowen ranch right where the marshal said it would be.

I rode up to the big house which wasn't all that big. A weathered bunk house was to the right and a well used barn and stables to the left dominated the place.

"You look in to sell that horse?" a voice called from the barn. "Should have checked the brand first."

A tough ranch hand in work clothes, a wide brimmed hat, and a hand on his hogleg stood with his free hand holding a pitch fork.

"The marshal in Alice Creek said it came from here. I was bringing it back," I said as friendly as I could.

"That's Tom Phillips's horse."

"His ridin' days are done."

"Why's that?"

"He had too many cards in a game up the trail. I tried to get him to just walk away."

"Tom's not much for backin' down."

"Not even when I emptied his pistols and let him go out the door."

"He reloaded and came back for another go, didn't he?"

"Got a couple of shots off before the barkeep gave him a double load of buckshot — more lead than he could eat."

"Sounds like Tom. Why are you goin' t' all this trouble?" the ranch hand asked leaning the pitchfork against the wall and stepping across to me.

"I was headed this way. Thought he might have somebody who cared or who might want to know."

"Not Tom."

I handed the reins over to the man.

"We owe you something for your trouble," a young woman's voice said from the porch of the main house. She was dark haired, wearing a calico dress and shading her pretty face with a small hand. I could tell instantly why Micah had fallen in love with her.

"Step down and eat with us?" she asked.

"Are you Mrs. Geneva Guymon?"

"I am," she said proudly in a melodic tone.

"I'm your brother-in-law, Joshua. One of Micah's other brothers."

She wiped her hands on her apron and beamed.

"Joshua!" She stepped off the porch as I swung to the ground.

I found myself in a hug from what turned out to be a shorter woman that I thought. She barely came up to my chest but I put my arms around her and gave her a squeeze.

"Micah around?" I asked not knowing what else to do or say.

"He's out with Pa *selling* some horses."

What that meant I wasn't sure. The way she said "selling" told me there was more to her statement than just the words.

"Ty," she said to the cowboy, "wash up and let's have lunch."

The ranch hand tipped his hat to the boss's daughter and moved off toward the barn with the bridle to Tom Phillips's horse in his hand.

"I could use a little cleaning, myself," I said as she reluctantly stepped back beaming at me.

"You don't know what it means to meet Micah's brother," she smiled almost to the point of tears. "He talks about you all the time."

"Then I'm glad he's away," I said. "It'll give me a chance to tell you my side of the story."

She had a rich infectious laugh.

"That's the man he's been telling me about."

"How did you come by Tom Phillips's gelding?" she asked as I took my reins and started to turn and follow the ranch hand to the barn?

"He -- ah -- came out on the wrong end of a bar fight up the trail. I was told the horse came from here."

"He did. Take care of your horse and Ty'll show you where to wash up. By the way, Joshua Guymon, this is Ty Ayres, our foreman."

I offered my hand to Ayers but he didn't take it.

"Name's Ty," he said and turned away.

"Thanks, ma'am," I said back to Geneva.

"We're family," she smiled. "I'm Geneva and you're Joshua. See you at the table."

There was something prophetic in her words but I didn't see it then.

CHAPTER 5

The cook was a large Mexican woman who liked tasting her handiwork and looked as if she had for years. The mess hall was attached to the main house. When she clanged the metal triangle that hung by a short piece of rope outside the door, a half dozen other working hands appeared and quickly washed up and took a seat at the long table.

I knew that a stranger at the table was nothing odd at a ranch table — cowboys ridding the *grub line*. These were unemployed and drifting cowboys who made their way across the country going from ranch to ranch looking for work or just headed to some unnamed destination. They'd stay alive only by the grace of the *grub line*, a free meal where ever they could get it. No decent ranch turned anyone away at meal time.

What was odd was that Geneva rose to her feet and announced to one and all, "This here is Micah's brother, Joshua. sure you make him feel at home." Then she sat down.

Usually even the boss's daughter and any other women folk would held with the cooking and feeding but Geneva sat at the table with the men for this meal. She was served first by the coosie. She knew to give

Geneva less than a third of what she heaped on the plates of the working men.

Juanita was the ranch house cook's name and she kept piling warm cakes of cornbread on the table which kept disappearing along with pots of steaming coffee. The food was good and there was plenty of it.

"Sorry I wasn't around when you and Micah were wed," I said to Geneva over the sound of men eating as much as they could as quickly as they could.

"Pa didn't think it was something to make a big deal over. He gave us $70 and told us not to come back until we were properly married and broke." She told the story with a smile but without embarrassment. "We went all the way over to Cheyenne in the snow. We found a bishop and real hotel. We'd still like to go to the Temple and be properly bound — but that's take time and money."

"That's what Micah told me in his letter," I told her.

"There's not much more to tell."

Finding a Mormon bishop instead of a frontier preacher said that both Geneva and Micah still considered themselves to be Saints. The standard practice would to have been married in the nearest ward house — but since none were near as they lived on the fringe of Mormon country — finding a proper bishop was the next best thing.

Then, too, couples wanted to be bound to each other for eternity — or for this lifetime if it was a second or third wife. The temple in Salt Lake City was, of course, the main place to accomplish this — but it could and was often done within the first year or so whenever a couple could find their way to any the church's temples.

The process took a full day and involved re-baptizing and checking ancestral records to bind other family members together — even family member who were not Saints and who had lived and died before Joseph Smith had his Revelations and started the Church.

"Wish you two had decided to head up north toward us instead of East. We could have helped you get to the Temple."

"At first Micah talked going to Salt Lake — and we intend to — to be bound — but we wanted to see somewhere else. We're not as faithful as we should be," she said lowering her head.

"Geneva," I said, "I'm far from any ideal Saint — but I do thing most of us do the best we can. You'll get to the temple. I'll see to it."

"Thank you, Joshua. That means a lot to me — to both of us."

"How long have you two known each other?"

"Goin' on two years now," she said wishfully. "I knew I loved him the day he rode onto the place. Pa kind'a took a shine to him, too."

"Folks always have taken to Micah. Part of it's what the Irish call the gift of gab. He can talk to anybody about anything."

"But the important thing is that in his heart, Micah's a good man. He tried hard to cover that up sometimes -- but that's who he is."

"You do know him well, Geneva. One thing I've never understood about my brother is why he wants to be something he ain't."

When Ty finished his coffee, he stood. That must have been an unspoken sign that the meal was over because all the hands got up then. They took their plates and cups to the washboard and piled them by the sink and followed Ty out the door and back to work. One cowboy hung back and walked over to where Geneva and I still sat.

"So you're Joshua?" he said with bit of a sneer.

He was about my size, broad shouldered with deep red hair.

"This is Amos Haggard," Geneva said without a lot of enthusiasm.

I stood and offered him my hand. He took it and tried to prove he had a stronger grip than me, but I held on and looked him right in the eye. After half a minute he yanked his hand away.

"Me and Micah been ridin' t'gether longer than he's been married."

"He must like his new arrangement a lot better."

Geneva had to stifle a laugh.

Haggard cut his eyes to her then back to me.

"You ain't as big as he likes to tell it."

"I've been cut down to size a few times."

"If it needs doin' again, I'm the man for the job."

"You be sure to let me know if you think we're comin' t' that."

"Oh, you'll know," Haggard tried to laugh. "You'll be the first t' know."

With that Haggard spun and left.

"That's the kind of *friend* Micah needs to be away from," Geneva said after Haggard was gone.

I watched her for a moment before I said, "The way you say certain words makes me wonder what you mean."

"What I mean is that Micah doesn't always know what's best for him."

"Does that include being with your father?"

Geneva looked me over for a lone minute before she said, "I hope I can trust you, Joshua."

"You can," I said. "So can Micah. And he knows that."

"Pick you out another horse, Joshua, and let's go for a ride," she said.

CHAPTER 6

All the horses in the corral were first class mounts. I tossed a loop over a dappled gray mare and saddled up while Ty grabbed Geneva's tack and her buckskin called Betty. I took my sheriff's badge from inside my vest and put it in the outside upper pocket. Something told me it would cause trouble if it happened to flash with a gust of wind.

Geneva came out of the main house in boots, a split riding skirt and a red top with her dark locks pulled back. When we were both in the saddle and headed away from the ranch, she took the lead and pointed us toward the nearby Aspen Mountains.

Everything was fully greened up even though there were tiny patches of the winter's snow to be seen if you looked for it. Both of our horses liked to run so we gave them their heads and they stretched out as we flew across the meadow.

When Geneva finally pulled up, we were at a fresh water pond and both mounts had good drinks.

"Are all your horses this good?" I asked her.

"A few even better. If they're taken care of," she said letting her hat fall back down her shiny hair until it stopped where the leather lace secured it around her neck. "That one you brought in, Tom Phillips's ride, he will need a week or so to get back to where he ought to be."

"I noticed he could use a good brushing."

"And some good feed. Tom never was one to much care how his horse was doing as long as it got him to where he wanted."

"How did you know him?"

"He worked here -- on and off -- mostly off -- for a year when Micah arrived."

"Phillips and Micah were close?"

"I wouldn't say that, but they did ride together."

"Was Amos Haggard there, then?"

"He came in with them. Haggard is lazy but he makes himself useful enough not to get fired by Pa."

"How about Micah?"

"He's always the first one up and on the job. He does what he's supposed to do -- and more. Pa noticed that right off."

"That's why he's off with you father now?"

Geneva sighed before she answered me. She looked around at the beautiful scene but I'm not sure she took in mountains or even noticed the soft breeze that slid across the water and cooled both us and our animals.

"Joshua, I feel like I've known you even before we met. Micah talks about you and everything he's ever said has been so good. That's why I wanted you to come out here and talk to me about this."

"About what?"

"There's something about Pa that's the same with Micah. Like I said, Micah's a good man -- so is Pa. But both of them seem to like being around men, mostly gentiles, who are truly of a different caliber. Bad guys. Amos Haggard, Tom Phillips and to a little less, even men like Ty. These are men who will cross the line at any moment and, I think, they're always looking for a reason to take that step."

"I didn't get that from Ty but Haggard certainly seemed ready to go at it for no reason at all."

"Haggard is a bully -- but I think he's seen enough of Micah to know when to back off."

"Micah can handle himself."

"And Haggard must know that. He never pushes Micah too far."

"What did you mean when you said your father and Micah were off *selling* horses? They're not?"

"This is no Zion, Joshua."

Zion was both Mount Zion in the Old Testament to us Mormons but also the place where we know believers lived in faith, harmony, peace and justice. Those who came to Deseret thought they were coming to Zion and sang songs proclaiming it. But the ideals of Zion were never fully achieved. We lived with Gentiles, non-believers, Indians and many who were only passing through on their way to somewhere else.

In strictly Mormon towns, settlements and outpost, the faithful always strove to achieve the goals of Zion. To many it was an ideal only to be reached in Heaven.

"Do you know what we do here?" Geneva went on.

"Breed and raise very good horses it seems."

"That we do -- but we -- we also *trade* horses with some people who are in a big hurry."

"Men on the run?"

"Sometimes. Do you understand the outlaw trail?"

"I know it's not a single trail."

"Right," she said. "And."

"Branches run from Mexico and Texas," I said remembering maps I'd seen, "-- up through Arizona, New Mexico, Colorado, Utah, Wyoming and spills out somewhere up in Montana. It goes through Robbers Roost and Hole In The Wall as well a bunch of places without names. Has great cover and look outs -- hard to find your way in or out unless you've been shown. You can see anybody coming a long way off -- plenty of time to get away."

"That's right. Do you know Micah's been down a lot of that trail?"

"Micah? Why?"

"Some of it he won't talk about. I know he wants to get away from it -- but it keeps drawing him back."

"Has he done something I should know about?"

"Before he came here. Good luck finding out what. If he won't tell his wife, I doubt he'll tell his brother."

"I'll bet you're right there."

"Could be we don't want to know. 'Least he doesn't want me t' know."

We didn't talk for a bit then I said, "Is that what he's doing with your pa now?"

"They never tell me -- but it scares me."

"They're leaving horses for some gang on the outlaw trail, aren't they."

"When they come back, they'll likely have as many mounts as they left here with -- only these will need a lot of rest and feed. Plus they would have made more money than the both sets of rides are worth."

"That's what this ranch is about?"

"Sorry to say, but yes. Oh, we sell a few head to the Army every now and then and a single mount to somebody from time to time -- but not enough to run a place this big this well."

Once more some silence passed between us before I spoke again.

"You've thought this through. What is it you want?"

"Joshua, you may be the only one who can do this -- but I need to get Micah and me away from here. I love my Pa but even he knows this isn't a good place to be."

"He'd likely let you and Micah to go without any trouble?"

"I think he does want what's best for me -- and here isn't it. I think if there were more or our kind, Saints, we'd all be better off."

"Thank you, Geneva. This couldn't have been easy for you to say. I'll see what I can do."

CHAPTER 7

Geneva told me how to get to this arroyo where a tree hung over the side. I was able to tie ten bottles to the lowest branch, turn my back, walk away and turn, draw and fire on them five at a time. It's one of the things I do to keep in practice with my .44.

As I shoot, reload, shoot again until all the bottles and the tops are all gone and I tie up another batch, my mind wanders.

Life is never straight forward, at least not to me and I'm thinking it's not for Micah. I seem to learn more by making the wrong choice than by being smart. From what I've seen most folks are like that. But I believe most are good at their core -- at least that's the way I tend to look at things.

Micah was the youngest in the family and I think in some ways he's still the baby of the family. But he and I have always been close -- except for the last few years. I think he was trying to find out who he was apart from me or even the rest of the family. Problem is, family is one of the most important things to us as Mormons. If we learned anything from Mama's reading to us all those years, it was how family should come first.

But Micah wanted to be wild, or part of him did. Thing is, he wasn't wild. He cared about people and couldn't abide a bully. When he left home, I knew he wanted to be alone and make some decisions without Papa, Mama, me or any of our brothers and sisters looking over his shoulder. He didn't write much and when he wrote that he was getting married in the middle of the winter, there was no way any of us could even get to his wedding. He said in his letter he knew that and didn't expect us to be. And, he would be married by the time we could even get here. It was the rest of the family who felt short changed.

Now that I had met Geneva I knew why he scooped her up as quickly as he could. She was a prize and a beauty. Like our Book of Mormon, she was the Pearl Of Great Price.

I had no business wondering if Micah was falling away from the church and the family. Geneva was a Saint but she didn't do much about it. They weren't even married in a temple, maybe because they couldn't get to one in the snow, but she was certainly the kind of girl I would have wanted for my brother.

Not being any more religious than I am, I go through the motions and attend weekly meetings, tithe, and put family first, I certainly can't judge Micah's faith.

I have my own problems with it. I know we're supposed to believe every word in the Bible and the Book of Mormon as true but -- a man living in the belly of a whale? It made a good story but was it true. Did it even have to be true? I know all fishermen are liars and thought this story came to be in the Bible only cause it had God in it.

How about God living on a planet near the star Kolob? I don't know where that is. But Joseph Smith wrote it so we were supposed to believe it. I don't even know if it's important that I do. Like most folks who live out doors as much as we do, I know most of the constellations and the names of the brightest stars. But Kolob?

I'm an elder in the church since I was 18. I'm also a priest and empowered to do good wherever I can. But I'm also very good with a gun. Partly it's because I practice -- but partly it's because -- it's a gift or a curse -- depending on how I use it.

After I hit the last five dangling bottle tops and reholstered my pistol, Haggard steps out from behind a corner of the arroyo with his hand on his pistol butt.

"You're pretty good, ol' son. But not too smart."

"Meaning?" I say watching him carefully."

"You're empty. If someone wanted to, it would be a good time for someone to pull on you."

"Why's that?"

"You're empty."

"You sure?"

"You been firing five shots at a time. That means you have an empty chamber where your hammer rests like everybody else."

"Could be I load an extra chamber when I'm out practicing just in case something like this happens."

"Not likely."

"It's not the kind of thing a smart man would bet his life on."

"Depends on what kind of betting man you were."

"This a bet you want to make?"

Haggard tried to stare me down then decided not to make the gamble. He slipped his holster thong back over his hammer, laughed and turned away.

As he went, I called him to turn around. He did and I drew and put a slug in the dirt between his feet. His face went white as I broke open my pistol, ejected the shells and changed cylinders for a fully loaded one, snapped my Schofield closed and holstered it again.

He swallowed and walked away. I waited to hear him ride off before I reloaded my other cylinder and rode back to the ranch.

CHAPTER 8

G eneva and I rode together the next day, too. I thought it was a good time to tell her about Micah.

"I need to tell you a story I'm sure you don't know."

She looked at me and said, "Go ahead."

"It's really a story that starts with me. Our father came from Germany and was a farmer there but became a rancher here. He was a lot smarter than most people gave him credit for -- including me.

"When I was 18 and Emma and I were about to get married he told me, 'Before you settle down and marry, you need to get away from here and have an adventure.'

"'An adventure? Papa,' I said. 'Yes. It does a young man good to stretch his legs and grow up a little on his own. A cattle drive would be a good thing, I think. And you should take Micah with you.'

"Micah was 16 then. Of course, he was all for it. What surprised me was that Emma also thought it might be a good idea."

"So you went," Geneva said.

"Yes. It was coming on to spring and Papa said he would hire a couple of local boys to do our chores and help him for the summer.

"Micah was as excited as I'd ever seen him. We got our things together and rode off for Texas. We joined up with a group of ranches that were doing their spring round up. It turned out we didn't know as much about cowboyin' as we thought. But we learned quickly. By the time we got on the trail we were pretty good hands. It ended in Wichita."

"Was it the adventure your father wanted for you?" she asked.

"We certainly found out how hot it was in Texas and Kansas in the summer. And dirty. We also learned how different people were from those we knew around home. Some of the men were failures who were just barely hanging on and some were always looking for trouble. There were a few who you could tell were going to do all right no matter where they ended up. Some others who were going to be drunks or get killed 'cause they liked to fight over nothing at all. We met a man who I think is likely a hell fire and damnation preacher by now. There were some who you knew you could always count on and others who would slack off every chance they got. Most were Gentile.

"We also saw our first 'soiled doves' in the saloons and even working out of wagons and tents along the trail.

"We saw more of life those three months than we might have taken years to come across up in the valley. I figured out how lucky we were and how good we had it to live with the kind of folks who decided to make their homes up where we did."

"And Micah?"

"I think he saw pretty much the same things I did -- except, being younger, I think he saw more adventure to it all than I did. We took our pay, stopped at one saloon for an hour and then headed home."

"Everyone was glad to see you back, I'll bet," Geneva said.

"They were. And we were glad to be back -- at least I was. Emma and I got married pretty quickly."

I rode on quietly until Geneva prompted me.

"What's the rest of the story?"

"We had already gotten our first few snow flurries -- the season was over and another long winter was ahead of us. But it turned out to be a hard year for more than a few of the folks. They needed things to make it through the winter, but they didn't have the money to pay for it. Mr. Oatly, owner of the general store, was a hard man. A

Gentile. Always thought he was better than any of us. I think he had failed at business a time or two before. He didn't give credit to anyone for anything."

"Must not have made him well liked."

"He didn't care. He wasn't married; had no children. He was a miserable man who saw other people as just a way to make money for himself.

"There were people already hurting but Mr. Oatly didn't seem to care.

"Then one early morning, there was a knock on Emma's and my door. It was Micah. He had a wagon packed full of goods. He had cleaned out Oatly's store and wanted me to go with him to deliver things to the people who needed it.

"I went with him just as it started to snow. The wagon tracks from town were covered up by the time we got to the first house. We made a list of who got what and everybody swore to pay us as soon as they could. We knew they would, too.

"We delivered everything to very surprised folks who we swore to secrecy."

"What about Mr. Oatly?"

"He was out of business. We had no sheriff or anything like that. He packed up his things and caught the last stage south two days later. Micah and I had eye-holes cut in two potato sacks and met the stage outside of town. The driver must have known who we were just by our horses, but Mr. Oatly didn't. When he got off the stage with his hands up, he was mad as hell. I held my gun on him while Micah climbed down and handed him an envelope full of cash. It was Micah's pay for the cattle drive and a little of mine. It more than covered everything taken from Oatly's store.

"Nobody said a word. Micah mounted up again and we rode off.

"By the end of the next year every cent had been paid off, back to Micah and me, just like we knew it would be."

"You're right, Joshua, Micah never told me that story."

"We never told anybody except Emma. And nobody ever said anything else about it."

"But everybody knew."

"Sure. But it's the kind of thing you don't talk about. I think it says more about Micah than anything else."

"It sure does," Geneva said.

"But I think he kind of liked the excitement of it all more than anything else. As soon as he had enough of his money back, Micah left. It was almost two years before we got even a letter from him."

"The letter about our getting married?"

"Yep. That's why I had to come find him."

We rode on a spell before Geneva turned to me.

"Thank you, Joshua. But I still think he -- we -- need to get away from here."

"If that's what you think."

"It is."

"Could take a while — but Star Valley is a wonderful place."

CHAPTER 9

A couple of days later my brother Micah and Stoops Cowen came home leading a string of hard ridden mounts. Micah was two inches shorter than me but had blond hair from our Swedish ma just like me. His build, however, was more like our German dad, lean and hard.

Micah only had eyes for Geneva. He swung down and ran to meet her on the hard packed dirt in front of the main house. He spun her around in his arms and kissed her like a man who truly missed his bride and had been away for a year. They were both gasping for breath when she pointed his attention to me standing on the porch. Micah had to look twice to believe his eyes, then he rushed over to me and we hugged and slapped each other on the back.

"Joshua, where did you come from?"

"It has been a while since we've heard from you. So Emma and I figured it was time I tracked you down and met your wife."

Micah pulled Geneva into a three way hug.

"How long have you been here?"

"A few days," Geneva said. "He's been waiting for you and Pa to get home."

"Who is this?" Stoops Cowen joined us. He was what was known as a tall, thin, drink of water who slumped his shoulders forward. His face was covered with a full bushy gray beard and his wiry hair tried its best to escape from under his dark, dirty hat.

"Pa, this is Micah's older brother..."

"The great Joshua?" Stoops chuckled good naturedly pumping my hand. "Well, welcome! Welcome!"

Without being told to, Ty had collected the ropes and bridles for the small herd of horses and moved them to the corrals.

"We'll have to kill the fatted calf," Stoops announced.

"Juanita is already ahead of you, Pa."

Stoops laughed. "She always is."

We had a great supper that night with plenty of beer to drink. Stoops was an enthusiastic host even if Haggard and Ty held back. The other hands seemed to enjoy the meal and the beer, but Haggard and Ty ate and drank but didn't participate in the gaiety.

The next few days I got to know Stoops a little and found I liked the man even if I knew he kept some things to himself. He appeared to have a genuine love for not just his daughter but for Micah, too.

I worked along side of Micah and saw that Geneva's assessment of him was precise. He got up early and worked hard all day long but never was shy about expressing his humor and love for life. The third day we were watching a little filly dart across a meadow when I commented about her to my brother.

"That's a runner there," I said. "The roan."

"I call her Rosie," he said with a smile of pride. "She's out of fine blooded pair.

"Is she broken?"

"She is -- very gently, too. I took special care with her."

"You have some plans for her?"

"Not really. I've just wanted to see what I could do if I bred carefully. Why? You got a notion?"

"Ever think of running her?"

"Racing?"

"We could take her out on the road and see. If she's as good as she seems, you might make a little on the side -- and you'd know what you have on your hands. For sure."

Micah watched his pony run for a minute and then turned to me and said, "Big Brother, I think you might not be as dumb as you look." He laughed.

"There are those who will argue that point," I said.

"Let's saddle her up and run her a few days and see if she's really ready. Do you know where to go?"

"I can make some notes. How about Geneva? Would she be okay with this? You've just come back."

"We'll talk. I think she'll like the idea." He took a breath and then said, "It might a week before I'm ready to leave -- you can understand that can't you?" He smiled.

"Just don't take too long. Remember I've been away from Emma for almost a month now."

"We'll get Rosie used to a racing saddle and a starting pistol."

CHAPTER 10

"What happened to Tom Phillips?"

Amos Haggard stood beside the corral gate I had just closed late one afternoon. His legs were apart and his arms were crossed over his thick chest.

"He had chance to walk away from a fight -- and he did -- but he had second thoughts seems like and he came back for more."

Ty walked up behind Haggard wiping the sweat from his forehead with the back of his shirt sleeve.

"That's sounds like Tom," Ty said. "I'm surprised he walked away in the first place."

"He wanted to go for his gun but he I think he knew he'd be dead before he ever cleared leather."

"You the one who backed him down?" Haggard sneered.

"I pointed out his options and his chances. He made his own decision."

"And?" Ty prompted. "You take his gun way from him?"

"Only long enough to empty the shells on the table. Then I gave it back to him."

"How about his hideaway?" Haggard knew Tom Phillips well.

"I emptied that one, too. But I gave it back to him and made him put it in his pocket."

"That must have pissed Tom off something fierce?"

"He was alive when he walked out of the bar."

"So," Haggard wouldn't let it go, "how'd he die?"

"He came back in shooting after he'd reloaded outside. He bit off more lead than he could chew."

"You kill him?"

"I was ready to -- but the barkeep served him first."

"Tom Phillips was a friend of mine," Haggard said bitterly.

"The way it was told to me, he didn't have many."

Ty spoke up. "That's true. Tom had a way about him."

"For better or worse he won't have that problem anymore."

"You're glad he's dead," Haggard said through clinched teeth.

"I gave him a fair chance to walk way and ride out. He picked his own path."

"He was a friend of mine!"

"So you said."

"If I'd been there, Tom would still be alive."

"It's doubtful. If I ever saw a man tryin' to get himself killed, Tom Phillips was that man."

Haggard unbuckled his gun belt and handed it to Ty who seemed to be waiting for it.

Without another word Haggard swung at me, a powerful right handed blow. I knew it was coming from the moment I saw him standing there waiting for me. It was just a question of what would spur him into action. I leaned back and let the punch pass by me and caught Haggard's foot with my own as his energy pushed him forward then on down into the dirt. He hit and rolled.

He realized I had been ready for him as he took his time climbing back up. I pulled my Schofield and laid it on top of the nearest fence post. He had wanted to fight me from that first day I met him at the table. All this about Tom Phillips had been an excuse even if Haggard and Phillips had been some kind of friends.

36

Haggard got himself set this time and had both hands up ready to go at it. Ty didn't do anything but stand back and watch.

I blocked the next punch with ease but, he caught me a glancing blow in the ribs.

Our father had been insistent that Micah and I learn how to fight. He had grown up with men who enjoyed wrestling and boxing as many farm boys in Germany did. The first thing he taught us was that getting hit wasn't the worst thing that could happen. You had to be able to take a punch and shake it off or you'd be done from early on.

Papa also taught us that if we could, get in close with a series of quick fast strikes. That would be more than any single round house punch no matter how well planned. I stepped inside of Haggard's reach and pounded his rib cage and knew I had taken part of his air with one punch before he bellowed and reached up to grab my hair. But I twisted back and whipped away from him.

Haggard was then like an angry bear. He swung with all his might in wild desperate strikes most of which I was able to dodge. He did catch me on the cheek with one strike that ended leaving little more than a scratch, but in his rage he opened himself up to several solid hits in the nose and even the side of his head.

What ended the fight was one frantic lunge that missed me as I ducked under his grasp and jabbed Haggard in the ribs with my elbow using my other hand to compound the force on the shot. I thought I heard a crack and the pain shook him as his knees buckled. It took Haggard to the dirt where his head thumped a gate post with the energy of his full weight. He tried to get up but the blow was too much for him and he slumped to the ground out cold.

I stepped over and picked up my pistol which I returned to my holster. I eyed Ty to see if he wanted to do something -- he didn't.

At supper an hour later I sat with my brother and his wife. Geneva turned my head to the side when she saw the mark on my cheek. She didn't ask and I didn't say anything. Micah was laughing with one of the other ranch hands and didn't notice.

Stoops arrived late entering from the doorway to the house and took his seat at the head of the table.

"Well," he announced as Juanita served him, "looks like Haggard's left us."

Questions came from some of the other hands and more than one said something akin to, "He won't be missed." Ty said nothing.

"When a man asked for what's due him and heads out without eating, he's made up his mind."

Scoops must have seen the mark on my face because he looked at me and asked, "You have anything to do with it, Joshua?"

"We had a few words out by the barn -- but he never said anything about leaving?"

"Were you the barn door he ran into?"

"Last time I saw him he was napping."

CHAPTER 11

"What do you want for your daughter?" I put the question to Stoops the first time we were alone a few days later as we herded a small group of horses to fresh pastures.

"I think she and Micah are pretty well set. They'll get this ranch -- all of it, every stick, creek, and pony -- when I kick the bucket."

"Will they also inherit the family business?"

"Horses are our business," Stoops said scratching his beard.

"I mean your real business," I told him. "Hiding, positioning and selling mounts to outlaws?"

"Who told you that?" There was more than an edge to his voice.

"Stoops," I said looking him right in the eye, "Geneva knows. Is that what you want to leave her? Is that what you want her involved in?"

The old man's face twisted into an angry, teeth clinched scoff and he opened his mouth to speak but didn't say anything. Instead the thoughts must have been flashing across his brain and he slowly softened and slumped in his saddle.

"She knows?" he finally said.

"I believe everybody knows. A town lawman up in Alice Springs first told me."

Stoops rode along a while without a word. When he pulled to a stop, I figured he'd come to some conclusion.

"I never committed any crime. Never robbed anyone, never shot anyone -- nothing."

"When you help those who do, you become a part of whatever they did. You have to know that, Stoops. You're too smart a man not to get it."

He spit.

"OK, damn it! But ...." he suddenly ran out of words.

"I may be wrong, Stoops, but I don't think that's what you really want to leave Geneva. You know it can't end well. What about when she has children? Is that the kind of thing you want for your grand-children?"

"Hell, no!"

"Then -- ?" I asked after we'd sat in the morning breeze a few moments in silence.

He looked away not wanting to face me, and I believe what he was seeing was himself.

"You have great horses here. I don't know that you realize what a great reputation your horses have. With some work, I believe you could become the first choice for the Army when it comes to mounts."

"The others who come to me -- who have been coming to me for years -- won't like it."

"Is it them or your daughter you care about?"

"There's no question there."

"Then you know what you need to do. Micah and I are going to take his Rosie out and see how she does racing."

"Saints don't race horses," Stoops said.

"They don't help robbers or bandits either."

We were quite for few moments.

"I'm not a model Saint, Stoops," I said breaking the silence. "Never pretended to be. In some way my folks are ashamed of me — but it's who I am. I like a little Leopard Piss every now and again. I also like coffee and a fair card game. I'm not above racing a good horse. If she wins, it could only help your reputation as a breeder of horses."

"Yeah, I see that." He took another breath before saying, "Oh, hell, I knew better than to do what I do. Always have."

"You've had your fun -- but it's time to do what's right by Geneva."

"I know you're right, Joshua -- but -- oh, nothing else matters."

He offered me his hand.

"Consider this," he said, "a new leaf I'm turnin' over."

I took his hand and we shook. I also noted a brightness in his eyes.

Micah and I pulled out leading Rosie a few days later. The route I first drew up started over west in Utah at Montpelier but Micah said he'd rather go the other way. Montpelier had been a kind of bad luck town for him, he said. So we headed east along the same path he and Geneva had taken for their honeymoon. He made a good point that a few out-of-the-way towns might be the best place to start seeing how Rosie would run.

We ended up in Rawlins on a Saturday. Farmers and ranchers filled the town and it wasn't long before races were organized. We got Rosie in the second running where she came in third. Running in a crowd was something that seemed to annoy her. She came in first in a race later in the day. This time she won easily. Micah and I were very happy with the way she performed.

We made camp down the road toward Ft. Laramie and made sure Rosie got a good rub down, and all the feed and water she needed. Micah and I had made $25 and learned that our roan could run well with others.

The following day we started south toward Denver and bigger races.

A single rider on a palomino, about thirty years old and wearing a broad brimmed sombrero, pulled out on the road in front of us from behind a boulder. He had a rifle under his arm.

We pulled to a stop without a word. The man wore a full mustache and hadn't shaved the rest of his face in several days.

"I think I will take the roan," he said moving his finger to the trigger of his rifle.

Micah and I exchanged looks.

Back to the rider I said, "No."

He cocked his rifle.

"I think, yes, señor," he said.

"You've not really thought this through, have you?" I asked him. "There are two of us -- you can get one of us but the other will get you before you can lever a second round into the barrel."

This made him reconsider his position but then he hardened his expression.

"Who will it be?" he said swinging his sights between Micah and me.

"Why not give me a try first?" I said when he was pointing his rifle toward Micah. I dove out of the saddle and rolled as the bandit swung back to me and fired. He hit me in the chest and it felt as if I'm been hit with a blacksmith's hammer. I hit the ground hard and rolled.

Micah pulled his pistol but the robber dropped his rifle and yanked his pistol and shot at Micah before my brother could get a shot off. The Mexican's shot missed Micah but caused him to twist out of his saddle. I got to a crouch with a pounding pain in my chest and had my Schofield out when I fired, catching the man in the side. My bullet threw him bleeding badly out of his saddle as Micah got to his feet and met me standing over the man.

The man's hands were empty at he clutched his side with both hands, his life's fluid seeping through his fingers. I grabbed the scarf he had around his neck and wrapped the Mexican's wound. He was gasping when I told him to hold the bandage as tightly as he could.

I got up on the back of his horse and told Micah to help the bandit into the saddle.

"What are you doing?" he asked lifting the man into a sitting positing on the ground.

"If we don't get him some help, he won't last the night."

"But he shot first."

"And he missed. Get him up here."

Micah did as I asked and the Mexican helped as much as he could, fitting his own foot in his stirrup. I helped the man into the saddle and tightened my left arm around him before taking the bridles Micah handed me. I started the palomino going and we headed back towards Rawlins.

CHAPTER 12

"Señor," the Mexican said from a bed in the back of the livery where the stable owner had patched the man up. "You are a Good Samaritan. Both of you are," he said including Micah. "I know the Bible story but -- you are Mormons aren't you?"

"We're still Christians," the stable owner said. "Why you damn gentiles don't understand that...." the round and bald man leaned against the door frame.

"Will he live?" I asked.

"Should," the man said starting to collect bloody bandages from beside the bed. "I've pulled slugs out of horses that were far worse than this hombre. They all lived. But who's going to pay for this. In the Bible ---."

I handed him twenty dollars.

"Will this cover it?"

He bit the coins one at a time and then nodded his head.

"It'll more than cover it."

To the Mexican I said, "You don't change your line of work you're going to end up at the end of a short rope with a long drop below you."

"Si," the man said. "Gracias. I am Armando Padilla. I would like to know who is the man who saved my miserable life?"

"Joshua Guymon," I said. "This is my brother Micah."

"I thank you both, señors."

Outside we mounted up again and started off for Denver once more. We were out on the road passing the boulder where the Mexican had confronted us when Micah said, "Joshua, how are you not dead? He hit you right in the chest."

I pulled out the severely dinted star from my upper vest pocket.

"What are you doing with that?" Micah asked slowly.

"Bishop talked me into being sheriff back home. I thought it wasn't much use here -- out of my jurisdiction."

"You never said anything about it. Why?"

"What was there to say? Does it make a difference?"

Micah rode on silently.

"Is there something I don't know, Micah?" When he didn't answer, I said, "Mama and Papa have been worried about you since you left. A year is a long time."

"I wrote when Geneva and I married."

"That's why I came looking for you. Mama insisted."

"I'm sorry," he said. "I should have never left. I was too young and…. I'm sorry."

"Whenever you're ready you should take Geneva and come home. We both know you're Mama's favorite."

"Joshua, I never…."

"I know you didn't. You were the baby of the family. You couldn't help it -- and that's the way things happened. It's all right. But Mama needs to see you."

Once more we rode in silence for a while. I noticed a tear sliding down his cheek but my brother had nothing to say. So I said, "I think I'll have to bang this dent out before I put it back on."

A while later Micah looked at me and asked, "Why haven't you said anything about Tom Phillips? You must know that I rode with him a while back."

"Yeah, I know. I figured you'd tell me when you were ready."

Micah merely nodded his head and we rode on to Denver.

~

Rosie became comfortable running in crowds, but she liked it best when she left them all behind -- which she always did. Denver was a good place for her. We made close to a thousand dollars in a week of races there before we moved on down to Santa Fe. Again the fine filly proved herself in every contest.

Next we took the Old Spanish Trail up across to Utah and Rosie established her worth in Moab, and Provo before we made it to Salt Lake. Once again we had the best horse running. With our pockets full we moved up to Ogden.

It was after the first win of the day that three men stepped up to us just as Micah dismounted.

"Micah Guymon," their leader said.

"That's me," Micah said cleaning his face with a handkerchief.

I recognized the man and his mustache.

"You're under arrest."

"Whoa," I said stepping between my brother and the town marshal, "aren't you off your range, Marshal?"

"Not anymore," he said pulling his vest showing a different badge than the one I'd seen him wear in little Alice Spring months before. "I am now a Deputy U.S. Territorial Marshal. Name's Larn Duffy."

The two men with him stepped to either side with their hands on their pistols.

"What's the charge, Deputy?" I asked.

"Murder."

"Who got killed? We've been on the road for almost two months -- Denver, Santa Fe, Moab, and Salt Lake."

"A bank teller -- over in Montpelier over a year ago."

"Who's your witness?"

"Amos Haggard."

The two men with Larn Duffy took a hold of Micah's arms. I noticed that Micah didn't seem to resist.

"Haggard," I asked still confused. "He's not a very reliable character."

"Normally, I'd agree with you, Sheriff," Duffy said to me, "but we have him as one of the gang who held up the bank there. He's admitted it but says it was your brother here that killed the teller -- a father with a wife and two children."

"Micah?" I turned to my younger brother. He hung his head and wouldn't meet my eyes.

The men pulled Micah away with them after they put handcuffs on him.

"Where are you taking him?" I asked.

"Sugar House Prison." Duffy faced me while the men moved off. "His trial will be in the Statehouse."

CHAPTER 13

W riting letters to Mama and Papa and another to Geneva as well as to Emma were about the hardest things I had ever had to do. I tried to be gentle in my telling what had happened, but what little Micah had told me wasn't easy to hear or believe about someone I love the way we all loved Micah.

I got a room at The Saint's Hotel in Salt Lake and found a lawyer named Nehemiah Schull who I was told after asking around for a full day was both honest and brilliant. He was a man who worked in his shirt sleeves with a gold watch chain that hung from his open vest over a slight swell around his waist from middle age. He wore spectacles to read but when he spoke, they either slid down to the end of his slightly crooked nose or up in his salt and pepper hair.

He rode out to Sugar House Territorial Prison south of town the next day. We met with Micah wearing black and white prison stripes. The room was small, hot, with chipped paint and only a table and four chairs. It also had one small high barred window.

"My boy," Nehemiah told Micah after I had introduced them and the guard had stepped out and closed the steel door, "no matter what you do, never lie to me. I'm on your side and nothing we talk about will go beyond these walls unless you give me your leave to do so. Do you understand?"

Micah nodded his head but kept his eyes on the floor.

"First things first," the lawyer said loosening his tie and taking off his coat. "Did you do it? The killing? Simply tell me yes or no."

Micah took a deep breath and looked up before he said, "No, sir."

"Good, then that gives me something to work with."

"I was there and it wouldn't have happened if we hadn't been trying to steal what wasn't ours," Micah said. "I was taught better and I knew better. For better or worst it was my fault."

"You've just stated the prosecution's case. But if you didn't do it, you shouldn't have to pay for it. Pay for what you did, okay. But not for that. Now, who did shoot the teller?"

Nehemiah Schull had his stack of papers open and a pencil poised to write.

"Haggard," Micah said after a moment. "It's just my word against his."

"But the territory made a deal with this Amos Haggard -- it was over another shooting." Nehemiah got out his specs and looked at the folder of papers. "He gets off easy with that one because he gives them you for the bank killing."

"Who was the other man Haggard shot?" I asked.

"A whoremaster in Vernal. Nobody will miss him. But Haggard did shoot the man in the back after being thrown outside for not paying for his -- pleasures.

"Now," Nehemiah said turning back to Micah, "tell me about the bank robbery."

"There's not much to tell. It was easy. We walked in and demanded money with our pistols out. They all handed over what they had. It was quick." Micah took a breath and closed his eyes remembering. "We were headed out the door. I was right in from of Haggard when he stopped -- for no reason -- and he aimed and shot the teller in the bank cage."

"The man didn't pull a gun of some kind out of his drawer?"

"No, sir," Micah said slowly shaking his head. "He still had his hands up and he was just standing there."

"And Haggard shot him for no reason?"

"None I could ever think of. We were done -- getting away was all we had to do. Mount up and ride off -- but Haggard shot him."

Nehemiah made some notes.

"Did anybody in town fire on you as you left?"

"No, sir. We galloped out of town, changed horses at a prearranged place and rode on and changed again. We were clear away."

"How much money did you get?"

"Four thousand, two hundred something."

"And nobody fired another shot?"

"No, sir, not a one. We never saw a posse or anybody else -- well, except for Scoops. Scoops Cowen? The man who left the horses for us?"

"That's where you met him?" I asked.

Micah nodded. "I don't want to get him into trouble over this. He had nothing to do with the shooting.

Nehemiah thumbed through his papers.

"Did you cover your faces -- in the bank?"

"Yes, sir."

"So nobody in the bank can identify you?"

"I don't think so."

The lawyer read some more as I studied my younger brother. Micah met my eyes and quickly turned away. I was still having a hard time believing it. My little brother who I had played with all my life. Of all my other brothers and sisters, Micah was always the one I was closest to.

"Is the pistol they took from you when they arrested you, yours?"

"Yes," I told Nehemiah. The Deputy Marshal asked for it. It was rolled up in his gun belt in his saddle bag."

Without looking up, Nehemiah asked, "It's the one you used in the robbery."

"Yes, sir. I won it in a poker game."

While Nehemiah read some more, Micah looked up and asked me, "Did you write Momma and Papa?"

"And Geneva," I told him.

"I don't want to see them here. Not like this."

"If they come," I said, "they will need to see you."

"In court. They let me wear my own clothes then. But not out here. I don't want them to come here -- especially -- at the end."

"Don't you give up, my boy," Nehemiah said putting his glasses away in a case. "I have some more work to do, but we're not done, yet."

Before we left, Nehemiah collected some other papers from the prison guards and went off too look at the evidence.

We rode back silently in his buggy. We each had our own thoughts. I was drawn inside. What would I do if they hanged Micah? I couldn't keep Papa and Geneva away -- I knew both of them must be on their way.

Sure enough Geneva and Papa had met and were waiting for me at the hotel when I returned.

CHAPTER 14

"He said he didn't do it," I told both Papa and Geneva. Papa looked as if he'd aged ten year since I last saw him in the Valley. "Where's Mama?"

"She is heart sick. She couldn't come. The rest of the family is taking care of her."

"Where's your Pa?" I asked Geneva who was still a pretty woman in spite of the burden pressing down on her small frame.

"Seeing to the horses, our buckboard and your father's wagon at a livery. He'll be along."

I got Geneva and Papa settled in their rooms. Papa was staying with me but I got both Geneva and Stoops rooms by themselves.

We all met Nehemiah Schull for supper in the hotel dining room. Everyone was impressed with the round man with the keen eyes. He asked important questions of us all but none of us, except Scoops knew about the robbery. According to Scoops there was something very different about Micah than the rest of the gang at the horse exchange point. Haggard had seemed very full of himself, but they quickly changed their saddles to their new mounts and went on their way.

A few months later Micah drifted back by the ranch and Scoops offered him a job. Haggard and the others had eventually come by and he took them on, too. But as far as Scoops or Geneva knew, none of them had ever pulled another job of any kind.

The rest of the next few weeks were spent with Nehemiah working on the case, writing letters and even taking a ride over to Montpelier and back. I went to see Micah every day alone while Papa and Geneva walked the town and got to know each other.

At night I saw Papa cry, but he was proud of the life he'd chosen and would live with any mistakes it involved. Both Papa and Geneva understood Micah's request for them not to come to the prison. So did I. The prison was a brick and stone fortress with nothing surrounding it. It was a depressing, gray and menacing place.

Micah seemed to grow thinner and paler each time I saw him; drawn, suffering from lack of sleep and brooding over what he had done, not just to himself but to Papa, Mamma, and Geneva. Some days he didn't have anything to say and we just sat across from each other in silence.

One day to give myself something to do I went to a blacksmith and borrowed his tools to hammer out the dent in my six pointed sheriff's star that had saved my life.

The day the trial began the proceedings took place in the dignified Salt Lake territorial court house -- three stories of white limestone plus a basement; turrets flanked the front entrance and judges' offices looked out on the lawn. Geneva and Micah embraced as much as his shackled hands would allow. Once the bailiff removed the bindings, they embraced again and he shook hands with Papa.

Opening statements were made by the prosecutor, a hard little black suited man with thinning hair named Bluford Dillard. He wore no glasses and spoke with a squeaky nasal voice through a small mouth.

"Cold blooded murder is among the worst crimes one human can commit against another, Saint or gentile. That is what we will prove --

that this man," he pointed at Micah, "Micah Guymon did kill an innocent father of two infants and the now widow of their young mother."

Micah closed his eyes at the description of the deed.

"By the time we are finished, gentlemen of the jury," Dillard went on, "there will be no doubt that the man seated there did this crime without a moment's hesitation for no reason than the mere fact that he is evil -- evil to his core."

With that flourish the prosecutor took his seat.

Nehemiah Schull stood and laid his spectacles on the papers on his table. He walked over to the jury and scanned them from one end of the jury box to the other as he spoke.

"If we can take the prosecution at his word, we should take my client out and string him up to the gallows. But the way our system works is that no man is presumed guilty of any crime until it is proven. The very reason you men sit here today is so, with an open mind, you can weight what you see and hear and decide in your own soul if Micah is the black hearted villain Mr. Dillard will portray him to be -- or if there is any doubt about the events and the way they occurred on that faithful day. All I ask of you is to not make up your minds until you've seen and heard both sides of everything. It is Mr. Dillard's job to convict the guilty, but it is your job to decide when a man is not guilty -- by a reasonable doubt. We believe that we are all innocent until it is proven that we are guilty. Imagine for a moment that it were you snatched up and thrown into Sugar House and called a murderer when you know none of it is true. It is a fact that Mr. Guymon was at the robbery -- we admit that -- but he did not kill the teller. Who among you have never stretched the truth or omitted a fact or two when trading a horse? Even Saints are not above stretching the truth a mite."

Some members of the jury cut they eyes to the left and right and then down to the floor.

"There was a robbery and a killing," Micah's attorney went on. "But there are other facts to this even you have yet to hear."

"Does it make make you guilty of being a horse thief -- because you left out a fact here or there or stretched the truth almost to the breaking point? Give this man," Nehemiah Schull indicated Micah sitting at the table with his head up now, "a chance just as you'd ask any jury to give you. No more, no less. A chance."

Nehemiah took his seat. Papa and Geneva had brightness to their eyes as Papa clutched my arm as a way of thinking me for selecting Micah's attorney.

Bluford Dillard stood once more and announced, "The prosecution calls Mr. Amos Haggard to the stand.

CHAPTER 15

Haggard was seated against the side wall on the prosecution side of the court. A prison guard unfastened shackles around his feet and hands before he strutted to the witness box and was sworn in. A hint of his usual sneer was on his face as he glanced at Micah before Bluford Dillard addressed him.

"Mr. Haggard, you have confessed to being a part of the bank robbery at Montpelier, Utah, in June of last year. Is that correct?"

Haggard nodded his head with a frown.

"Will you please speak up, Mr. Haggard?" Dillard said.

"Yes. I was there."

"And a part of the robbery?"

"Yeah," he said reluctantly.

"And was Micah Guymon a part of the robbery."

"Yes," Haggard answered without a pause.

"Anyone else?"

"Tom Phillips."

"There were four men. Who was the other?"

"I forget."

"You swore to tell the whole truth, Mr.Haggard."

"I forget."

"How long have you known Micah Guymon?"

"Maybe two years."

"Have you ever known him to shoot anyone else."

"Nope. Just this once."

"Tell us about that time."

"We was done," Haggard said. "Finished. We'd taken all the cash they had -- even a watch, two rings, and some coins from the people in the bank when we started for the door."

When the witness didn't continue, Dillard prompted him, "Please go on."

"That's when he did it," Haggard said as if that was all that was required.

"Did what, Mr. Dillard?"

Haggard took two breaths before he said, "He -- Micah -- turned back and shot the teller."

"What was the teller doing?"

"Just standing there -- his hands up like we told him."

"Anything else you wish to add, Mr. Haggard."

"No -- but I didn't know why he did it. There was no reason. Micah was just a mad dog, I guess."

"Objection," Nehemiah Schull shot to his feet. "The witness is characterizing the accused without justification."

"Objection sustained," the hefty judge said pointing his gavel at Haggard.

"If it's not a fact, the witness will keep it to himself."

Haggard didn't say another word.

"The prosecution yields the witness," Dillard said taking his seat.

Even before he stood again, Nehemiah Schull asked, "Why are you here, Mr. Haggard?"

"Why? To tell people what Micah did."

"You're just doing your civic duty as a good citizen?"

"Yeah, you could say that."

"Are you a Saint, Mr. Haggard? Do you follow the ways of Joseph Smith?"

"No. I ain't religious at all."

"And you are a bank robber? Willing to steal money you did not earn or save?"

"I admitted that."

"And you decided to turn yourself in because you felt guilty about the robbery?" Nehemiah was now on his feet but still at the table.

"Well -- no. Not exactly."

"The exact truth is that you've made a deal with the prosecution, isn't it?"

"Objection," Bluford Dillard bolted to his feet. "The defense is leading the witness."

"Am I, Mr. Dillard?" Nehemiah asked. "What have I asked that is not true?"

Dillard didn't have an answer for that. Instead he appealed to the court.

"Your honor, please."

"The question is well within legal bounds, Mr. Dillard. Continue Mr. Schull."

"All right. Mr. Haggard, we've heard your testimony. But you've still not told us why you are here. Have you ever been involved in other shootings?"

It was clear to everyone in the courtroom that Amos Haggard didn't want to answer this question. He licked his lips and squirmed before he could force the words out of his lips.

"Yes," he said.

"Recently -- in Vernal?"

Bluford Dillard was again on his feet but he had no words to say.

Nehemiah turned to his legal colleague. "Is this a question the prosecutor wants to answer?" Dillard dropped to his seat with his teeth clinched.

"It appears it's all up to you, Mr. Haggard. I'll ask you once more, have you been involved in other shootings -- particularly in Vernal?"

"Damn you!" Haggard said under his breath.

"Louder, if you please, Mr. Haggard, I'm not sure everyone on the jury heard you."

"Yes. I shot a son-of-a-bitch in Vernal?"

The judge shouted at the witness, "Mr. Haggard, you will keep a clean mouth in my court."

Haggard took the rebuke but didn't say anything.

Nehemiah continued, "Recently?"

"A week ago."

"Where did you shoot him?"

Dillard now had a proper objection. He bolted to his feet. "This has nothing to do with the matter at hand, Your Honor."

"If it please the court," Nehemiah said calmly, "the relevance will become clear in just a moment,"

"It had better be quickly," the judge said.

Nehemiah turned back to Haggard.

"Where did you shoot this man?"

"In front of a whorehouse."

The jury all laughed and the judge banged his gavel.

"No," Nehemiah said, "I meant were in his body?"

With only a little embarrassment Haggard said, "Between his -- in his chest."

"Isn't it more accurate to say that's where the bullet exited? Didn't the bullet enter the man's body *between* his shoulder blades -- in his back?"

Haggard didn't answer.

"Your honor can you instruct the witness to answer. We can get the town marshal who arrested Mr. Haggard to tell us if need be?"

"Okay," Haggard said. "I shot him in the back. He deserved it. He was a pimp who threw me out of a damn whorehouse."

"This is the second time I caution the witness to watch what he says in my court!" the judge shouted at Haggard.

Looking at the jury Nehemiah said, "Does anyone deserve to be shot in the back? Unable to defend himself?"

"That's what Micah did to that teller," Haggard said.

"Micah shot the teller in the back?"

"Same as. The man couldn't defend himself."

"Which, by your own testimony is the way you deal with others, Mr. Haggard."

"I tell you I didn't shoot him!" Haggard demanded.

"What gun did you use in your most recent shooting?"

"My own, why?"

"What is that gun?"

"It's a Colt. The great equalizer."

"Tell me about it?"

"It's a nickel plated .45."

"A pretty nice gun. Is this it?" The lawyer picked up Haggard's pistol on an evidence table."

"Looks like it."

Nehemiah took each of the bullets out of the pistol before he took it to Haggard. "How long have you owned it?"

"Three, maybe four years. Yeah, this is mine," he said handing it back to the lawyer.

"Do you ever loan it to anyone else?"

"Hell, no. The only way you get your hands on my gun is when I'm dead."

"You had it with you but didn't use it during the bank holdup in Montpelier?"

"No. I mean, yeah, I had it but ... The only one who fired that day was Micah -- when he killed the teller."

Nehemiah put Haggard's weapon back on the table and turned back to him.

"Can you tell us about the deal you've made with the prosecution? When do you go on trial for that most recent shooting?"

"Sometime soon. I don't know exactly."

"What will be the charge?'

It was a moment before Haggard quietly said, "Manslaughter."

"Manslaughter?" Nehemiah asked clearly to the jury. "Not murder? Manslaughter which means no malice -- even possibly accidental?" Back to Haggard Micah's attorney said, "How about this robbery you admit participating in? When do you stand trial for that?"

Glaring at Nehemiah, Haggard said, "I have immunity for that."

"Immunity. No trial because you will no longer be charged with that crime?"

Haggard didn't respond.

Back to the jury Nehemiah said, "What would someone do to get a deal like that? Someone who shoots people in the back? Remember this when you consider Mr. Haggard's testimony.

CHAPTER 16

The prosecution's next witness was Montpelier county sheriff Melton Eggleston, a thirty-three-year-old freckle faced brute with blond, dirty hair. He was a man very impressed with his position and authority. Each of his answers was almost bellowed when he spoke. He recounted the events of the robbery in Montpelier step by step including the organization of a posse which had no luck in trailing the robbers. Once Bluford Dillard finished getting out all of the information he wanted, he turned the witness over to Nehemiah Schull.

Geneva, Papa, and I sat in the court room behind Micah watching and listening. This whole affair was out of our hands and we felt totally helpless.

"You were not the chief law enforcement officer of the county at the time of the events you're telling us about were you, Sheriff?" Nehemiah asked checking the pages on the table before him.

"Uh -- no," Eggleston said quietly but loudly enough to be heard."I was the deputy."

"And where exactly were you when the robbery was taking place?"

There was a moment of silence in the court before the witness said, "I was performing other duties."

"Exactly what duties, Sheriff?"

"Ah -- supervising the eviction of a rancher for the bank."

"Was this near the bank?"

"No. It was two miles outside of town."

"Am I correct in stating that you were not a witness to the robbery yourself?"

"No," Eggleston said, "but I've studied the files and talked to everyone who was there."

"Can you identify who it was that shot the bank teller."

"I know it was that man there," he said pointing at Micah.

"As an honest lawman, Sheriff -- someone who was not even in town much less in the bank, how can you say that?"

"Because the other robber said so!"

"You are willing to stake your reputation on the word of a back shooter?"

The sheriff thought this over for a moment and then said, "No."

"Then, Sheriff, do you know from what you have seen with your own eyes who pulled the trigger on the pistol that killed a member of your town in that robbery?"

"No, I can't" Sheriff Eggleston admitted without the bluster he had begun his testimony with.

When prosecutor Dillard called his next witness, it was the wife of the bank clerk, Tobias Pemberton, who was killed in the hold up. Mrs. Claudine Pemberton was a plain but neat woman dressed in black. Her age was stated as twenty-four. She was not a witness to the events of the robbery or the murder of her husband either, but she did earn the sympathy of the jury by her testimony.

When Bluford Dillard passed the witness to Nehemiah Schull, Micah's attorney stood respectfully and stated, "We have no questions for this witness, Your Honor. Please dismiss Mrs. Pemberton with our condolences."

The lady was surprised that Nehemiah had nothing to ask her but she did not accept his inclination of sorrow because she clearly thought he represented the man who had murdered her husband. She scowled at him as she stepped down and took a seat in the court.

We were surprised when Mr. Dillard then rested the prosecution's case. Nehemiah quickly stood and called his first witness.

"The defense asks Mr. Micah Guymon to take the stand."

Micah walked to the witness box and raised his hand to be sworn in.

Nehemiah first question surprised us all.

"Mr. Guymon were you involved in the hold up of the bank in Montpelier, Utah?"

As instructed Micah turned to the jury and said plainly, "Yes, sir, I was."

"Was Amos Haggard part of the crime with you?"

"Yes, sir," Micah said without hesitation.

"Under oath Mr. Haggard has testified that you are the one who shot Mr. Tobias Pemberton during that robbery. Is that true?"

Still facing the jury Micah said, "No, I did not."

"Can you think of a single reason why the jury should believe you?"

Micah sighed and said, "No, sir. I don't know I'd believe me either if I was on the jury."

"But you are adamant that you did not do that shooting?"

"Yes, sir. I was a thief -- but I've never killed a man in my life."

"Then let's look at some other things," Nehemiah said as the crossed to the evidence table. He hefted a blue steel, wooden handled, octagon barreled pistol with double hammers. He ejected one of the cartridges from the gun and set it down on the table. "Is this your pistol?"

"Yes, sir."

"Is this the one you used in the robbery."

Micah hung his head.

"Yes, sir."

"Did you fire it in the bank, as you fled from Montpelier or at the posse who followed you?"

"No, sir. Not once."

"Your witness, Nehemiah said to prosecutor Dillard.

Dillard was licking his chops to get at Micah.

"Let me reaffirm for the jury that you have admitted you were a part of the robbery of the bank in Montpelier where bank clerk Tobias Pemberton was murdered."

Micah nodded his head as he firmly said, "Yes, sir."

"You helped plan and execute this nefarious crime and were a part of it from start to finish?"

"I'm not sure what -- *nefar---* whatever that word is you said means -- "the whole court room laughed, "--- but I was in on that robbery from start to finish."

Dillard recovered his pompous dignity and spoke over the tittering of the crowd as he said, "Including the murder of the bank clerk?"

"No, sir," Micah, said, "I didn't do that. I didn't shoot anyone."

"Your fellow conspirator, Amos Haggard, has told us you were standing beside him when you fired your gun."

"Amos Haggard is a liar and a bully. He always has been."

"You should be proud of your actions, Mr. Guymon. You did this whole crime! Be a man and own up to it!"

"I've admitted what I done," Micah said. "But I won't admit to something I didn't do." He looked around Dillard at the widow sitting on the front row behind him, "Ma'am, I'm as sorry as I can be your husband was killed, but as God is my witness, it wasn't me that did it!"

"Liar!" Dillard yelled getting red in the fact.

Nehemiah got to his feet as the prosecutor fumed. "Your Honor, my colleague has asked his questions and gotten sworn testimony to them. If he has no other questions, I would like to proceed with the defense."

The judge asked, "Do you have any other questions, Mr. Dillard?"

Reluctantly Dillard sat saying, "No more questions."

"The witness may step down. Mr. Schull, call your next witness."

"The defense calls Doctor Hector K. McGlasson.

CHAPTER 17

Neither Papa, Geneva nor I knew the Doctor McGlasson Nehemiah called to the witness stand. The pot bellied man wore a black suit and vest. He had receding white hair, a small mustache and a cleft in his chin.

Once he was sworn in and took his seat, Nehemiah approached him.

"Dr. McGlasson, you are the official County Coroner of Summit County including the town of Montpelier, are you not?"

"I am."

"How long have you held this office?"

"Oh -- I have to count to be exact but over twenty five years."

"Were you the one who examined the body of Mr. Tobias Pemberton the murdered bank teller in the robbery."

"Yes, I was."

Nehemiah collected a sheet of paper from the evidence table and handed it over to the physician who pulled out his spectacles from his lower vest pocket.

"Is this the report you wrote as you conducted the autopsy of Mr. Pemberton?"

"It is. I signed and dated it down here." The doctor pointed to the bottom of the page.

"Can you please refer to your findings and tell us what was the cause of death."

"A single gunshot wound to the chest."

"What was the weapon?"

"I could only say that witnesses in the bank said that the robbers all carried pistols and no rifles. So I surmised he was killed by a pistol."

"Could you determine the caliber of the pistol?"

"Not from the wounds."

"Wounds. I thought you said he was shot only once."

"Yes, but there was an entrance and an exit wound."

"So the slug did not remain in the body?"

"No. It was recovered from the back wall of the bank."

"Can you determine the caliber from what was recovered?"

"Not exactly. I could give you a range but the bullet was too deformed to make identification positive."

"I see," Nehemiah took the report from the doctor and passed it to the jury for them to look at individually.

Next Nehemiah stepped to the center of the court and addressed his question to the witness.

"Dr. McGlasson, how many post-mortems have you performed over your career?"

"Less than a hundred. We don't generally do that unless there has been a suspicious death or we know the deceased was the victim of a crime."

"Like a murder?"

"Like a murder, yes."

"Have you seen bullet wounds -- not just fatal but otherwise as well?"

"Good, Lord, yes. More than a third to a half of my practice has involved gunshots -- deliberate and accidental."

"And the ones on Tobias Pemberton?"

"What about them?"

"Is it possible to determine if it were accidental or deliberate?"

"There's no way to tell that. A bullet is rather indiscriminate. Like the rain. It falls on the just and the unjust alike."

Nehemiah thought for a moment before posing his next question.

"Is there anything you can tell us about the projectile that caused these particular wounds."

The doctor considered his words for a moment before he said, "They was caused by a weapon of considerable size -- .44, .--- 44-40 or .44-70,--- or a .45."

"Excuse me, Doctor, but if it was .44-70, wouldn't it have to be rifle?"

"That is correct. So if it were a pistol, it would have had to be a .44 or a .45."

"And we know there were no rifles in the bank," Nehemiah said as he went to the evidence table and picked up two bullets there and brought them to the witness stand.

"Of these two bullets, Doctor, in your experience, which would be most likely to be the one to cause the injury you saw on the body of Mr. Tobias Pemberton?"

Papa, Geneva and I exchanged looks. We thought we knew were this was going.

The doctor examined the two cartridges and set the smaller one down on the ledge in front of him. He held up the larger and said, "It would have to be one like this -- a .45."

"Are you sure?" Nehemiah pressed.

Dr. McGlasson picked up the smaller bullet.

"This is too small. It couldn't do the damage I saw on the victim's body. And the slug wouldn't be as big as the one we dug out of the wall of the bank."

"Thank you, Doctor," Nehemiah said taking both cartridges over to the jury to pass around.

"Your witness, Mr. Dillard," Nehemiah said as he took his chair again.

The prosecutor seemed to be confounded by the testimony. He stepped over to the jury and retrieved the doctor's report from the last jury member. He looked over it and then looked at the bullets making the round of twelve men sitting in the jury box. Dillard returned the report to the evidence table and tried to think of something to ask the witness. Finally in frustration he took his seat saying, "No questions."

The judge, his narrow face pinched said, "Do you have another witness, Mr. Schull?"

"I do, Your Honor," Nehemiah said getting out of his chair. "The defense calls Mr. Bartley Webb."

From the back of the court stood a man in his fifty's. He wore what must have been his Sunday suit and he carried a ledger of some kind under his arm. He had a long full beard and rough but narrow, strong fingers.

The man took the oath with a Swedish accent and sat down.

"Please tell the court your occupation and how long you have been at it," Nehemiah said.

"I am a gunsmith. I apprenticed in the old country over forty years ago. I have had my own shop ever since then. Today I own the Bartley's Firearms – Guns Made and Repaired."

"In Salt Lake?"

"Yah," he said.

Nehemiah went to the evidence table picked up Micah's pistol and brought it to the witness.

"Do you recognize this pistol?"

Bartley took the pistol, opened it and clicked each cylinder until ten cartridges fell into his lap. He double checked it to be sure it was empty. Next he turned it over and examined the number on the bottom of the grip. He opened his book and found an entry several pages back.

"Yah," he said, "this is it. This is the only one of its kind I have ever seen."

"Can you tell us what it is?"

"It's a Welch twelve shot revolver. It has two hammers," he demonstrated pulling one to half cock and the other to full. "It was originally a percussion cap revolver -- .36 caliber."

Nehemiah said, "Originally? What is it now?"

"It's been modified to take cartridges -- still .36 caliber. It is still single action -- it must be cocked before it can be fired, by the trigger," he held the pistol up so the court and then the jury could see it. "The trigger has two positions -- one for each hammer."

"Who did the modifications?"

"I did." Bartley handed the pistol to Nehemiah who in turn passed it over to the judge. "Two years ago."

"For whom did you do the modifications?"

"Mr. Micah Guymon. He paid me $22 dollars for the work."

"Will it fire a .44 or .45 caliber shell?"

"No," he said. "They are too big. They will not fit into the chambers."

Nehemiah took the pistol from the judge and handed it to an open mouthed Bluford Dillard at the prosecution table. After Dillard had examined the weapon, Nehemiah took it back and handed it to the jury. As he took his seat once more, Nehemiah said, "No more questions, Your Honor."

CHAPTER 18

S toops had made the decision not to come to court in case he was recognized or named by Amos Haggard and named as the supplier of horses to many of the men living and working on the Outlaw Trail. Because of that he was not there with his daughter, Geneva, Papa, and me as we watched the end of the trial.

Prosecutor Bluford Dillard did his best to paint Micah as a murderer. Micah had admitted to being one of the bandits and so he was an admitted thief. Where the small mouth, squeaky voiced lawyer had his biggest problem was trying to prove his case based primarily on the testimony of Haggard.

Dillard tried to rage like a hellfire, but there were open snickers from not just the court but even the jury before he demanded the jury convict Micah as a cold blooded killer.

When it was Nehemiah Schull's time to deliver his final argument, he put his spectacles on the top of his head as he stood.

"Gentlemen of the jury," he began, "it is Mr. Dillard's job to get justice not just for the widow of Tobias Pemberton but for the Territory of Utah. But when justice comes in the form of depending on the testimony of the likes of Amos Haggard," he motioned to Haggard who sat in his shackles against the side of the court room between two prison guards, "-- well, some fields are just not meant to be plowed."

Nehemiah returned to his desk and picked up some of his notes he had taken all during the trial. Referring to them he said, "Mr. Haggard has admitted being in the bank at the time of robbery as has my client. However, because of the agreement he has made with the prosecutor's office, he will receive no prison time for that crime and only a manslaughter charge for an admitted back shooting of a man in a totally unrelated event. But the nature of that second crime, the place, the circumstances under which it took place, and the other party involved tell us a great deal about Mr. Haggard's character --- the character which is supposed to have provided reliable testimony in this case."

Geneva gripped my hand and Papa's hopefully.

At the evidence table, Nehemiah picked up the two pistols and showed them to the jury.

"You gentlemen have had a chance to examine both these pistols --- both of which we know were used in the bank robbery." He put the weapons down and picked up a .45 and a .36 caliber bullet from the table and carried them between the thumb and forefinger of his two hands as he stood in front of the jury. "You know from the doctor who examined the body of the bank teller what kind of round it would have taken to make the wounds which killed young Mr. Pemberton, and you know it could not possibly be the gun of my client. You also know that Mr. Haggard told us he would never lend his pistol to anyone else."

Nehemiah held up the .36 caliber cartridge from Micah's pistol and then the .45 slug from Haggard's Colt.

"Which of these would have caused the deadly wounds we heard described?"

Our lawyer returned the ammunition to the evidence table before he turned back to the jury.

"Two men --," he gestured to Micah and then to Haggard. "You have heard from the mouth of both and can judge for yourself the kind of men they are. Micah Guymon is a Saint who lost this way but has now found his way back. He is married and is working to provide for his wife and future family. Amos Haggard has no faith anyone can find. He has no life behind him but one of crime and shootings --- and none ahead of him but prison and more violence. Surely you can see that as well as I can.

"So what do you do? My client has admitted and stands ready to pay for the bank robbery he participated in, but this young man is no killer. You have seen him and heard him. He is humble and has learned from his past. But does that past include murder? Can you see this young husband cold bloodedly taking the life of another for no reason? Now, look at Amos Haggard and ask yourself the same question.

"Gentlemen, do your duty," Nehemiah implored them, "-- but do it with honesty and compassion. You know who you can believe and who you cannot. You know who can be saved and who cannot."

As Nehemiah sat, Papa patted him on the back and I saw tears in Micah's eyes as Geneva openly cried quietly.

Outside while the jury deliberated, Geneva told Stoops what had happened and Papa asked me to go with him as he approached the bank teller's widow, hat in hand.

"Mrs. Pemberton," he said to the plain looking woman dressed in black.

She turned to Papa not knowing what to expect.

"I am Micah Guymon's father," Papa said, "and this is my son, the sheriff of Star Valley, Joshua."

I removed my hat and nodded to her.

"I do not know what you are doing to keep yourself and your children going."

"We have nothing," she said. "We live in the house my husband bought but it belongs to the bank and they are not, yet, demanding money --- but they will. I take in sewing and washing. It is all I can do."

"Well, no matter what is decided inside," Papa went on, "I want you to know that you and your children will never have to worry. You have a home with us and everything you could ever need."

The young woman was shocked and covered her mouth as she tried to take in what Papa had just said.

"When you get to know us, you can decide what you want. I am an old man and I have a wife --- but I will marry you if you will accept me. You and your children will become my heirs. Joshua and his wife will also look to your well-being."

"That is a promise," I spoke to her for the first time, "from me as well."

"It is a Mormon way and we will abide in it with honor, respect, and love."

The woman had tears streaming down her face as she was overwhelmed with relief.

CHAPTER 19

Haggard was already on his way back to prison in a barred wagon by the time the jury came in less than a half hour after adjourning. The jury found Micah guilty of robbery but innocent of murder. The judge sentenced him to seven years for the robbery and gaveled the trial to an end.

Micah leaned across the railing and took Geneva in his arms as the deputies stepped up and began to shackle his legs.

"Geneva, I am so sorry."

"I will wait for you."

"Seven years? It's too long and it's not fair to you."

"It's no longer than Rachael waited for Jacob," she told him through her tears. "You are my husband and I will wait for you."

When the officers took Micah's hands to shackle them, he turned to Papa.

"I have brought you shame, Papa. Can you ever forgive me?"

"Pay for what you have done, my son," Papa said. "You are young and you can still have a good life."

To me Micah said, "Will you look in on Geneva from time to time?"

"She is welcome to come and live with us if she likes," I told him.

"Yes!" Geneva said instantly as if this was the solution she had hoped for.

"And I will come visit you, Micah, and I will bring Geneva." This seemed to please my younger brother greatly.

One last kiss from Geneva and the guards said, "Okay, let's go."

Nehemiah Schull had become a family friend. I was able to pay him out of the racing winnings Micah and I had accumulated, but he seemed embarrassed and looked down running his hand through his salt and pepper hair when Papa and I thanked him with all the sincerity we could generated. He told us that if we ever needed a lawyer again to come see him and if he wasn't the right man for the job, he'd direct us to someone one who was.

Stoops took Geneva home and promised to have her packed when we returned. Papa and Mrs. Pemberton, she asked us to call her Claudine, took his wagon with Micah's horse and our race horse, Rosie, trailing behind to Montpelier. I rode beside them.

We filled Papa's wagon with the belongings Claudine and her late husband, Tobias, had acquired. We also met her two children, a straight haired but clear eyed girl of three named Polly Elizabeth and a one and a half year old boy named Paul Joseph. The boy was sandy haired and sucked his thumb.

It was supper time when we pulled into Stoops Cowen's ranch. Juanita had plenty of food as usual and the children were soon asleep, little Paul in his mother's arms and Polly leaning against Geneva. The two ranch hands and Ty, the foreman, said nothing during the meal and Stoops seemed sad but resigned to the fact that his only child, Geneva, was going away with us in the morning.

The leaving the next day wasn't emotional at all. Stoops had come to terms with what was happening, and made it his business to check that everything on both Papa's wagon and the one Geneva and I would take were tied down well for the journey.

Geneva gave her father a last hug and said, "I'll stop by every time I go to visit Micah."

"You do that," he said is if they were talking about the weather. "I'll be here." This last remark told me that the scruffy bearded old man had decided to get out of the horse supplying business for outlaws, but he didn't want to make an announcement about it.

Geneva wore a gingham dress and bonnet which couldn't hide her beauty. She held her head up and looked ahead as I climbed up beside her and took the reins.

It was shortly after sun up when we pulled out of the Cowen ranch and we pushed hard all day, stopping only for a trailside lunch and to rest the horses before we went on.

Geneva and Claudine got on well and Geneva proved to be a wonderful hand with the children who took to her. Papa was deferential to Claudine in every way, a perfect gentleman as he always was, but exceedingly kind even playful with her daughter and son. I saw Claudine looking at Papa once as if she couldn't believe such a person had come into her life when she needed him the most.

As we passed through the nameless town, I recalled the card game and shooting which I thought of as the beginning of everything that had brought us back this way. I thought it was all over as we left the few buildings behind --- but I couldn't have been more wrong.

When Geneva and I pulled into Emma's and my place, she was standing on the high front porch of the house I'd build us up so we wouldn't be covered in drifts from the winter snow. That she was expecting was a wonderful shock and as I kissed her and twirled her in my arms I was as gentle as my emotions would allow.

"Why didn't you ever tell me in any of your letters?" I asked placing my hand on her belly.

"Because I wanted this," she laughed and I swung her around again.

She was still laughing when she pulled away and went to Geneva who stood at the bottom of the stairs.

"You would be Geneva," she said and took the young woman in her arms like a long lost sister. Geneva gave back as big a hug as she got.

"Joshua said you were pretty, but he didn't say you were beautiful. Micah must be so proud."

Geneva blushed.

"Thank you for allowing me to come," she said.

"Of course," Emma said beaming, her soft red hair shining in the setting rays of the sun. "We are family and you will always be welcome here. Don't think twice about it."

CHAPTER 20

I spent the summer adding a room to our house for Geneva. Emma had hired some excellent hands to help out running the ranch and I kept them on.

Twice a month Geneva and I would make the trip down to Sugar House. Papa went with us only twice before the first snows fell. Our last journey to Utah for the year was in mid-October when Geneva and I were caught in a blizzard and had to spend a night in Alice Springs huddled on chairs around a potbellied stove in the general store for a night and a day.

From what Micah told us, he went out of his way to follow all the rules and did whatever any of the guards asked. He saw Haggard across the dining room and sometimes on work details but they never spoke. Haggard had been given the same sentence, seven years for the back shooting of the whore master as Micah had for the robbery. It was the deal Haggard had reached with the prosecutor for his now proven false testimony against Micah for the killing of the bank clerk in Montpelier.

Emma and Geneva became like sisters sharing the chores and Geneva taking the full load when Emma grew exhausted with the growth of the new life she was carrying.

Claudine Pemberton was coming out of her shell with Mama's good humor and the growing love her children displayed for both of my parents. On New Year's Day Bishop Douglas performed a wedding for Claudine and Papa for what is called "for time only". She had been sealed in marriage to her now dead husband Tobias forever and remained so. She and Tobias would be together in heaven. Papa and Mama were still sealed for eternity.

At the end of the ceremony Papa signed a new will Nehemiah Schull had drawn up. It made Claudine, her daughter and son Papa's legal heirs. Mama stood beside him as he signed holding Paul on her side and Polly by the hand. My three brothers and three sisters were there with their families and were happy for the peace and security Papa had given this newest member of our family.

My duties as sheriff consisted of my breaking up fights in the Ox Head saloon, a gentile owned in town, from time to time and getting Orian Akin home when he had drunk himself into unconsciousness. He was called out three times in church for his behavior.

There were also disputes about cattle ownership, broken fences and trampled crops. Nothing violent but there were matters that needed a law representative.

Orian Akin came to me one day in late July and asked for my help.

"This drinkin' thing is more than God has given me the strength to handle alone," he told me his big shoulder and his head hung in shame. Together we went to the Ox Head and instructed the bartender to serve him nothing but beer from now on no matter what he demanded -- and no more than two in one day. We also went to the Sorenson mercantile and told Mr. Ezra Sorenson to sell Orian nothing with alcohol in it with the doctor standing there with him.

By the new year Orian was back on the true path and was once more a proud and righteous family man.

At Papa and Claudine's wedding I had asked Bishop Douglas if it weren't time to see if the folks wanted somebody else to be sheriff. He'd appointed me without any kind of election. He stroked his long gray beard and looked me up and down. Then, in his deep voice he said he'd bring it up come Sunday.

Sure enough after services that week he asked the congregation to keep their seats for a few minutes more.

"I took it upon myself to appoint Joshua Guymon as our sheriff two years ago. Recently Joshua asked me if it were time for someone else to take on the job. I want to put it to you all now. Do you want Joshua to continue as our lawman or are there others who are interested in the task?"

The people in church discussed it among themselves and it was Orian Akin who stood up and spoke.

"It was Joshua who helped me when I didn't know what to do. I don't know anybody else I could have asked who would have been as steadfast and honorable as he was to me." Orian also smiled that crocked smile of his before he said, "And I don't know a man in this valley who is better with a six gun or who could take him in a fight. Plus we all know he's honest. All together aren't those the things we want in anyone wearin' a badge?"

He sat and the congregation all applauded.

"Looks to me," Bishop Douglas said, "like there's your answer, Joshua. You're our sheriff."

I nodded my head in acceptance.

We got letters from Micah all winter and the whole family kept writing him. Geneva, Papa and I made our first trip of the New Year to Sugar House in late March. Micah told us he had been made a trustee which was a sign that he was paying his debt to society by keeping all the rules.

Before we could make our second trip, a late season storm snowed us in once more. While we awaited the next visitation date, we received a letter from Micah telling us not to come -- not until the roads were clear. But he also told us to make sure we were there on May first because he was to be pardoned and released on that day.

CHAPTER 21

The story of Micah's pardon came to us in his next letter.

As a trustee Micah was given more freedom than other prisoners, but he wrote that he made a point of not abusing this privilege. He did use his freedom and access to obtain books and mail for prisoners in the prison hospital.

He was shocked to be invited to the warden's office one day where the warden, Branch Hallenbeck, told Micah he had visited a couple of times with Nehemiah Schull in Salt Lake. It seems that Nehemiah and Warden Hallenbeck had been friends for many years. The warden said he was the one who sought out Nehemiah because he had been getting reports from prison guards about Micah. The good words from Nehemiah were what convinced Hallenbeck to make Micah a trustee a year earlier than any other prisoner had ever earned the position.

Still Micah was assigned to regular work details. He didn't mind because of the chance to get outside the Sugar House walls. The first major project of the year, cleaning a drainage ditch which would help channel the snow melt run off, was when the incident happened. Amos Haggard was a part of the work detail from the beginning.

The third afternoon when the work gang was back to work after lunch, Warden Hallenbeck drove by in his buggy with his daughter, a petite twelve year old named, Effie Anne. He stopped to talk to one of the guards on horseback. The inmates kept on working with hoes and shovels.

Moments later Haggard was standing between the ditch and the guard with a pistol in his hand. Where he got the gun, no one ever knew. Someone must have hidden it in the ditch for him but how long he had it before this moment was a mystery.

Haggard ordered the guard to drop his shotgun and for the other guard to do the same. The guards hesitated and Haggard shifted his aim to the warden. Both guards then dropped their weapons. Then Haggard ordered the warden and his daughter out of the buggy. They climbed down. Haggard changed coats with one of the guards and told the Warden to put his trousers on the buggy seat.

Micah wrote that he had eased his way closer to the group when Haggard suddenly swung his aim to him.

"Don't you take another step, Guymon! I'll kill you where you stand!"

Micah stopped.

Haggard stepped up and grabbed the warden's daughter and pulled her to him as a shield.

"Leave Effie Anne alone!" Warden Hallenbeck pleaded with his hands still up in the air. "You can take the buggy! No one will stop you!"

"Oh, I know no one is going to stop me," Haggard laughed pulling the child with him toward the buggy. "Tell the guards to empty their shotguns!"

"Do it," the warden commanded.

Both guards slowly picked up their pump shotguns and pumped out all the shells.

"Throw the guns in the ditch!"

They obeyed.

Haggard made another move toward the buggy.

"Wait!" Micah called.

"I told you not to move," Haggard said taking aim at Micah.

"If you take the girl, they will hunt you down like a dog!"

"What do you care? You'll be dead!"

"You have a better chance without the girl and without the buggy. Take the guard's horse, unhook the one on the buggy and take that one with you. You'll get a better start and make better time."

Haggard held his aim on Micah but thought about what was said.

"Unhook the warden's horse," Haggard ordered Micah.

Micah did as he was told and handed the bridle to Haggard.

"Now bring me those empty shotguns," he said to Micah. "Pump 'em twice so I know they're empty."

My brother followed Haggard's demands, located the two shot-guns and holding them by the butts, he carefully pumped both to prove they were empty. Micah held both the guards shotguns and said, "Let the girl go. Here," Micah laid the weapons on the ground in front of Haggard. Haggard looked around and saw that no one was moving.

He pushed the frightened girl to the ground at the warden's feet. Hallenbeck took his child in his arms and turned his back to Haggard to shield her.

Haggard picked up the shotguns and crammed them both into the rifle boot on the saddle. Then he climbed into the saddle keeping his pistol trained on Micah.

Slowly he make his mount back up and then turned around and headed west toward the Outlaw trail. As he started to go, Haggard turned around and then fired two shots at Micah. Micah went down and Haggard rode off.

Micah told us he had been hit in the left leg but it was only a flesh wound. He said that Haggard's shot attracted the attention of other guards with a nearby work gang clearing brush. By the time one of the other group's guard arrived, Micah had a make shift bandage on his leg.

The warden told the men to hook up a horse to his buggy and march Micah's group and the other prisoners back to Sugar House.

Haggard got away and no one but Micah was hurt. Haggard would have had even more time had he not taken time to shoot at Micah -- but that's the kind of vicious man he was.

Micah wasn't badly wounded and was fully recovered by the time we were there to pick him up for his release.

CHAPTER 22

The great news about Micah made everyone happy -- even Claudine who was Papa's new wife and the widow of the murdered bank teller Micah was acquitted of killing. She had come to believe at the trial that Micah was not the assassin of her first husband and the father of her children. She, like everyone else in court, believed it was the lying outlaw Haggard who had just escaped, shooting Micah in the process.

Geneva was anxious to go see Micah but God seemed to have other plans. The day before we were supposed to leave, Emma gave birth to Ester Octavia. Emma had a long and difficult labor because our daughter was a big, healthy girl with bright red hair.

It was Geneva's decision to stay with Emma while Papa and I took Rosie, the filly we had raced in Colorado and up into Utah, for Micah to ride back home from prison. Papa wanted to stop at Stoops Cowen's to tell him about his daughter before we rode on. We ended up spending the night and riding on in the morning. He asked that we stop again on our way home so he could shake Micah's hand and give us Geneva's horse, Betty, to take back to Star Valley.

We met Warden Branch Hallenbeck who was waiting with Micah and lawyer Nehemiah Schull outside the prison when we rode up.

The warden was a ruddy faced, small man who carried himself straight and proud. He shook out hands with a firm grip and even patted Micah on the back.

"We don't ever want to see you back here," he told Micah as my brother stepped into the saddle.

"You won't, Warden. I have a wife and a life outside of Utah."

"And not returning to Utah," Nehemiah explained, "is one of the key stipulations of Micah's pardon and release."

The warden handed the rolled up pardon tied in a neat red ribbon to Micah who put it in his coat pocket.

"Thank you, Warden. You're a fair man."

"And you, Micah, are a brave one. I owe the life of my daughter to you, young man."

"I couldn't have done anything less," Micah said tipping his hat.

"Gentlemen," Nehemiah said to us all as he walked to his horse and tightened the cinch before climbing aboard.

"Warden," Papa tipped his hat and I did the name.

"Oh," Warden Hallenbeck said turning back to the front door, "Micah, I don't believe anyone ever asked you about the money from the bank in Montpelier."

"I don't know, Warden," Micah said without hesitation. "I never wanted anything to do with any of it."

"Did the others spend it?"

"No, sir, they buried it."

"Do you know where?"

"No, sir. I didn't want to know. I didn't go with them when they buried it."

The warden nodded. He seemed to understand and opened the door without another word.

We turned and left, Nehemiah to Salt Lake and us east to Wyoming.

The ride was a good time for Papa, Micah, and me to talk.

"Have I paid my debt, Papa?" Micah asked.

"Your true character showed itself when you stood up to Haggard and saved the warden's daughter. Made me proud of you, son. The

Territory of Utah has forgiven you with your pardon. I couldn't do anything less."

"Thank you, Papa. Joshua?"

"It's good to have my brother back," I told him.

As we rode, I told Micah he was welcome to stay with Emma and me as long as he needed. He wanted to know all about his new niece, Ester Octavia. I told him it was time he started his own family. He said he and Geneva would get right on it. We laughed together.

We got into the Cowen ranch and pulled up beside the wagon Geneva and I had used to take her to the valley. I called out for Stoops.

"He's out in the south pasture," Ty said from the barn door where he stood holding a rifle in his hands. "He'll be back, directly."

"Why the rifle?" I asked.

Ty swung the rifle up and shot Micah out of the saddle without another word.

Papa leaped to the ground to see about Micah.

By instinct I pulled my pistol and fire at Ty. He yelled as my shot hit him. I dove to the ground and got another shot off. The shot hit the barn door but I couldn't tell if my aim was true or not.

"How's Micah?" I called over my shoulder. When Papa said nothing I turned and looked. Micah's eyes were open to the sky but still. A growing spread of blood came from the wound in the center of his chest.

"Papa?" I asked.

When Papa looked up at me, I knew Micah was dead.

I charged the barn looking for any movement to indicate where the ambusher had gone. Sliding to a stop against the outside wall, beside the partly open barn door, I listened for the slightest sound. I broke open my Schofield pistol from the top and put a cartridge in the usually empty chamber where the hammer normally rode; then I replaced the two spent shells with new bullets from my gun belt. I cocked the hammer and waited only a moment more.

Having heard nothing, I yanked the barn door open and plunged inside hitting the ground and coming up on one knee.

Ty was splayed back against a stack of hay clutching his neck which was squirting blood. His rifle was in the dirt beside him.

I stood and stepped over to him.

"Why did you kill Micah?" I demanded.

"He – he - stole - our - hidden money," he gasped out through gurgling blood now in his mouth.

I kicked the rifle away as I stood over him. I turned and Papa was standing at the open barn door, Micah's blood on his hands.

"Why?" Papa asked.

To Ty I said, "Micah didn't take your money. He didn't even know where you hid it."

An odd expression crossed Ty's face before he looked back at me.

"Oh -- damn. I -- kilt -- the -- wrong -- man."

A last breath seeped out of him; then Ty sagged and was still.

CHAPTER 23

Papa and I built a pine wood casket for Micah in Stoop's barn. Stoops had his other ranch hands take Ty's body out to "anywhere you can dig a hole and plant the son of a bitch."

We wrapped Micah tightly in two blankets and put him in the box. The next day Papa drove Stoops' wagon while Stoops and I rode behind leading Geneva's horse, Betty.

As we pulled into my place, Geneva rushed out and stopped on the top step of the porch when she realized what she was seeing. She fell back to the porch wailing in instant grief. Emma hurried out with the baby in her arms and she, too, grasped what Geneva had understood without having to be told. At that moment, the how and why of the thing didn't matter.

The whole valley turned out for Micah's funeral. Bishop Douglas gave the eulogy, but I don't remember a word of it. The whole family was going through the ritual but it was a blur. Emma and I heard Geneva crying through the night.

When I woke the next morning, I found Emma in the kitchen packing supplies in my saddle bags. I slipped my arms around her from behind and asked, "What are you doing?"

"You're going after Haggard. We both know it. I'm getting you ready."

I turned her around and kissed her. This woman knew me so well.

While I dressed, she made breakfast. When I returned to the kitchen, Geneva had little Ester in her arms and Geneva tried to smile. I didn't know what to say beyond, "Good morning."

She sat at the table still holding my daughter and said, "My daddy's going with you. I expect he's already at your gate waiting."

I looked from my wife back to Geneva not understanding completely what was going on.

"I talked to Daddy after the service," Geneva said. "He wanted to know what he could do -- and I told him he could go with you."

"I didn't make up my mind for sure that I was going until last night," I told the pair.

Emma said, "Joshua, what else can you do? Of course, you're going after Haggard. He must have dug up the money and taken it. He didn't shoot Micah -- this time."

"But he did when the escaped prison," Geneva picked up the thought. "And he tried to get Micah hung for the killing in the bank *he* had done."

"Haggard didn't pull the trigger that killed Micah -- Ty did -- but Haggard's hand was on that gun as surely as if he were standing there." Emma set the breakfast plates on the table and took her seat across from me. "When Bishop Douglas asked you to be sheriff of the valley, he also appointed you a Danite -- an avenging angel. Your skills with a gun and at protecting people -- it's who you are."

Geneva rocked Ester in her arms. "You may not have decided what to do, but we all knew."

Stoops was waiting at the gate when I rode up just like Geneva said he's be.

There were no words to say, we just turned toward his ranch and rode.

~

Stoops broke the silence after a couple of hours on the trail.

"I figure the roost," meaning Robber's Roost in Utah, "would be the place t' start. They'll put up with most anything there -- except murder. Haggard won't have told them about the bank clerk, I'm sure."

Further on he said, "We need to get you another horse. They'll recognize Tom Philips' ride from a long ways off -- and they won't give us any trouble."

"They know your horse," I said without looking at Stoops.

"Sorry t' say. 'Don't know why I ever got involved with those types. Excitement, mayb'? But look at what it's led to."

There was nothing I could say to Stoops that he hadn't said to himself.

A while later he said, "Micah was the best man Geneva ever come across. He was a better man than me -- or most ever'body else I know -- 'cept you, Joshua. You're the kind of man both of us should have been more like."

We rested out mounts in the nameless town where Tom Phillips had died. We had a beer in the same saloon. Toby, the skinny barkeep knew who I was but neither he nor his whore, Gert, said anything when we ordered and paid for our drinks. Stoops and I sat at a different table than the one where all this began.

"On second thought, we ought to try Brown Hole first. It's closer. Depending on what we find out there, we can either head for the Roost or back up toward Hole in the Wall." We sat in silence a while before Stoops spoke again, stroking his beard as he thought. 'Best let me do most of th' talkin'. They know me -- 'least who I used t' be. That Stoops they'll talk to."

What he was saying made sense. From Stoops' ranch on the Green River the Outlaw Trail went south into Utah. From there it either went on thru the Utah Territory and or split into Colorado or Arizona. Depending on the branch you took, it then traced a path to New Mexico or Texas and into Mexico. The other end went north back into Wyoming up towards Hole in the Wall then on to Montana.

No matter which way we went, we would have to be ready to fight every minute.

The ol' Stoops was a silent partner in crime to those to rode that trail. He had supplied good horses and asked few questions over the years. He'd been well paid for his trouble and his silence, but like he had said, he was reaping what he had sown -- but so were the ones he loved.

CHAPTER 24

The reason the Outlaw Trail had never been settled was mostly because the land was hard and there was no give in the terrain. Green as it was from the melting snow of May, the scrub brush and grass would soon struggle in the long hot summer days for lack of water all along the twisting, knotted, and winding path very few men rode. High buttes squeezed the trace to narrow passages which then opened up to wide, jagged, and harsh meadows up against towering stony peaks. From the high points you could see for miles in all directions, but there were no straight paths anywhere.

Stoops and I made our way to the Uinta Mountains generally keeping the Nest Fork of the Bear River to our left.

Brown Hole had been a mountain man hold up site and later the location for Fort Davy Crockett. But that was long ago. The mountain men and the fort had vanished and this place became a good hideout for outlaws. There was a hand pulled ferry across the river and a tattered old store and bar among the few surviving wood and mud buildings. Most had gone the way of the buffalo but had been wiped out not by hunters but the ravages of hard winters and damaging summers.

We pulled up to the store/bar and loosened our cinches so our horses could blow. There were four other mounts hitched to the rail out front.

In the dark interior the store counter was also the bar. Stoops and I put silver coins down and asked for whiskey.

"Stoops," the barkeep, an apple round man with a pockmarked face produced two glasses and an unlabeled bottle.

"Not that crap, Jarvis" Stoops said. "The real stuff."

Jarvis made a sour face and exchanged the bottle for another.

"Who's your partner?" he said and poured our drinks.

Stoops didn't look up but watched Jarvis pour.

"My son-in-law."

"You ain't Micah," the barkeep said turning to pour my drink.

"Micha's dead," Stoops said and tossed down the drink. "Another."

Jarvis closed his mouth which seemed to hang open most of the time.

"'Thought he was in Sugar House."

"He got a pardon."

"Pardon? We heard Haggard had killed him."

"He tried," Stoops said. "He missed."

"Then what happened?"

"They pardoned Micah 'cause he saved the warden's daughter from Haggard." It was a moment before Stoops said bitterly, "Ty Ayres killed him. Ambushed him from my barn."

"Where's Ty, now?"

"In hell," I said my first words.

Jarvis put the bottle up and left us alone with our drinks.

The bar was silent until a chair creaked behind us. Stoops looked under his arm at the sound and then returned to his drink. Under his breath he said, "The Clancy brothers and Bull Guthrie. Mean and nasty as they come. I've seen Bull crush a man with just his arms.

"Never did hear your friend's, name," said a voice from the dark across the room.

Stoops slowly turned with his drink in his hand.

"Cleave. That you?"

"Yep. Woodie and Stover are with me. And I'll bet you can smell Bull over there."

"As soon as we walked in," Stoops said taking a sip.

"And your partner?"

I turned around.

"I'm Micah's brother -- Joshua."

A chair grated on the planked floor as Cleve stood and stepped into the light streaming through a crack in the roof. He was stout and hairy about medium height. He wore two guns hung low in a fancy pistol rig. His hat was hanging on his back by a string around his neck.

"You send Ty t' hell?" he asked.

"Proud t' say I did."

Two more chairs pushed back. Cleve's brother stood up still mostly in the dark. But I could make out two figures much like Cleve. The major difference was that they wore only one six gun a piece.

"I kind of liked Ty," Cleve said.

"He ever kill a brother of yours?" I asked.

"Nobody messes with the Clancy brothers and walks away from it."

"He messed with my brother -- and he didn't walk away."

"We're not here to mess with you, Cleve," Stoops said.

"It ain't your choice, Stoops. You bring a lawman in here ---"

"Lawman?" one of the brothers asked.

"A sheriff from Star Valley, as I hear it," Cleve said.

"He's not here on law business," Stoops tried to calm a situation that wasn't going to go but one way no matter what.

"Don't matter," the other brother said. It could have been Woodie or Stover -- not that it would make any difference. "Law dog is a law dog."

"You boys know the rules," Jarvis said, "no killin' here or you don't *ever* come back."

"There's killin'," Cleve said, "and there's all but killin'. It ain't the same."

"Can you at least do it outside?" Jarvis pleaded to deaf ears.

"Stoops," Cleve said, "we're goin' t' leave you out of this so you can tell the tale."

"I ain't stayin' out," Stoops said finishing his drink and putting it down on the bar.

"Then Guthrie might take hold of you so you don't get in the way."

The bulky, vat chested hulk got up from across the room and approached.

"Ever had your plow cleaned, Joshua?"

"Not in a few years -- it was by a better man than you," I told him.

He was fast and caught me with a left in the side before he bore in with a powerful right I blocked with my forearm. Both brothers closed in quickly as Guthrie grabbed Stoops and lifted him off the floor. I ducked and the two boys pounded their fists into each other's and yanked their bruised and injured hands back with a yep.

I came up in Cleve's face and battered his ribs with solid shots with both hands. He clenched and stepped back giving me enough time to draw back and connect with his chin in a blow that cracked bone and teeth. He fell back as I whipped around and caught one brother in the nose squarely and sent blood flying.

The other brother tried to punch with his remaining good hand but it was poorly aimed and lacked much behind it. I stepped under it and came down with both hands clinched together at the base of his neck and shoulder. He folded like a drenched rag.

Cleve fumbled for one of his pistols, but I planted the toe of my boot in his ribs and he rolled over in so much pain he couldn't do much else but moan.

The brother with the cracked fist and bloody nose needed only one more clout in the face and then he was done.

The hulk was applying all of his frustration to Stoops who was flaying in desperation for breath. I used my boot again; this time between both men's legs, but the toe sank into Guthrie who instantly released Stoops as he slumped forward with his hands going for his crotch. With both open palms I smacked his ears with all my strength. He yelled and straightened some -- enough for me to put a fist into his mouth, shattering teeth in the process. He hit the floor like a stunned buffalo.

I pulled my pistol and twisted around to find Jarvis trying to raise a shotgun from behind the bar. He froze when he realized I had the drop on him. He eased the double barrel to the floor and raised his hands.

"What do you want to know?" he asked.

CHAPTER 25

The Clancy brothers and Bull Guthrie were known stage coach bandits and were known to be accused of more than a few rapes over the years. Stoops and I packed them out on their own horses, slung across their own saddles except for Bull who we had to tie sitting up roped to his saddle horn and his stirrups.

They were all moaning in agony as they bounced along the trail for hours.

By two hours after sun up we were nearing Liberty. Still inside Utah we weren't surprised to see Larn Duffy with his big mustache and a U.S. Deputy Marshal's badge when we pulled into the sheriff's office in the emerging town.

"Friends of yours?" Duffy asked rocking his chair back to four legs from where he'd been leaning against the wooden wall.

"You interested in the Clancy brothers and Bull Guthrie?" I asked tossing the deputy marshal the bridles.

"As a matter of fact," Duffy said walking from horse to horse and lifting up each head by the hair and paying no attention to the whimpers from each man. "Where'd ya' find'em?"

"They was there just sittin' around at Brown Hole," Stoops said when I didn't answer.

"Brown ...." Duffy didn't finish the name. "Well, you boys have been busy. Did you find what you were lookin' for?"

"Not yet," Stoops said. "But we ain't through, either."

"Go have some breakfast and come see me 'fore you leave. There's some money on these boys' heads."

"We're not hunting bounties," I told Duffy.

"No, I figure you're looking for Amos Haggard. I heard what happened at your ranch, Stoops. It's not hard to put two and two together." He turned toward the building and yelled, "Sheriff?" as he cut Bull out of his knots and let him fall to the ground. "You have some unwelcome, nonpaying boarders out here!"

"Go on and eat," he said to us once more. "But do see me 'fore you ride out. I might have something that'll help."

Stoops and I exchanged looks then pulled away.

"The Vegas House has the best food in town," he called after us. "It's on your left."

Stoops and I ate. He rubbed his ribs a couple of times.

"Bull would have killed me if you hadn't stopped him," he said.

"I was thinking I'd need your help loading them up."

The old man grinned and chuckled once until it hurt. We ate the rest of our meal in silence.

Back at the sheriff's office, Deputy Marshal Duffy was back in his chair beside a slight man with sharp eyes wearing a sheriff's star and a cross draw Colt. The other two men who had been with Duffy when he arrested Micah at the racing ground leaned against the wall. I noticed that one of them was a half breed.

"Sheriff Hutchingson, this is Sheriff Guymon and Stoops Cowen."

We all nodded to each other.

The marshal stood and stepped off the boardwalk to the hitching rail where Stoops and I sat in our saddles. He looked at me.

"I have two men here," he indicated the men leaning against the building. "Either would be good to ride the river with." To the half breed on his left he said, "Lute Quickdeer, is the best tracker I've ever known. He could follow a spider across water."

"I appreciate the offer," I said. "But Stoops and I need to do this ourselves."

"I kind'a figured that would be the way you'd feel. Then take this," Duffy said reaching in his pocket and tossing me a Deputy U.S. Territorial Marshal's badge.

"Thanks," I said moving to pitch it back to him, "but no thanks."

Duffy held up his hand.

"Keep it with you. I know what you're going to do."

"We're not going to arrest Haggard ...."

"You're goin' t' kill him. Yeah, I know. So, keep that badge. Haggard is wanted dead or alive."

"So why do I need this?" I asked.

"You don't -- but it will help in case anybody asks any questions. Besides, we could always use another deputy."

"You know I'm Mormon and I live in Wyoming."

"Yeah."

"If it comes to backing your government," I held up the badge, "or my faith -- you know where I'll be."

"I know. 'Wouldn't expect anything different."

We held each other's gaze for a moment.

"You're a good man, Joshua Guymon. The rest of it is more politics than religion. I don't trust politicians any more than you do."

I thought about it a moment and then looked at Stoops. He nodded at me. I pocketed the badge put didn't pen it on.

Duffy stepped back to his chair, sat and leaned back against the wall.

Stoops and I pulled away and rode steadily out of town.

A half hour down the trail, Stoops asked, "You that good a tracker?"

"I'll do," I said.

We rode the rest of the morning and into the afternoon without a word as we headed towards Robber's Roost.

CHAPTER 26

"I'm glad you didn't take Duffy up on his offer of help from the breed," Stoops said.

"You know him?" I asked as we rode down the red walled canyons and past towering buttes.

"Not him, no. And it ain't 'cause he's a breed. I know you can't pick your folks. Hell, Geneva would be much better off if she could have picked. She sure as hell wouldn't have picked me. No, it's Utes I don't trust."

"The few I've known are good people."

"Mayb' now. But I saw two uncles, an aunt, my ma and paw hacked to death by a war party -- oh, must be forty years ago now. But it was like yesterday t' me. I'll never trust a Ute or any part of one."

"Well, I figured we needed t' do this ourselves," I said.

"Damn right!"

Through the twisting canyons we rode. Without Stoops as a guide, it would have taken me months to find my way, especially since recent rains had washed tracks clean. It took us most of the day to make it to the roost.

Robber's Roost was the Chenowith ranch, a sprawling place between the steep walled canyons within ridding distance of three rivers: the Colorado, Green, and Dirty Devil. It was part of a wild stretch of acreage crisscrossing miles of hidden draws and almost inaccessible territory. As the afternoon sun began to move behind the gigantic canyon walls, the rocks and land turned to alternating shades of purples and greens and deep shadows.

We rounded a smooth sculptured wall, carved centuries ago by rushing water and wind, and pulled up with the ranch house a half mile away. This was not a place you approached unannounced. Together Stoops and I stepped down and walked forward slowly leading our horses.

"Dillman Chenowith or somebody stayin' with him will be watching us. Could even be one of his daughters, Enid or Trudie. 'Never could tell them apart. Let's take our time."

And so we did, strolling easily. We saw a blink of reflected light and I tensed.

"Easy," Stoops. "It's more likely a spy glass than a gun barrel. They see us and see we ain't comin' in hard."

After a bit Stoops called, "Hello, the ranch!"

A man's voice answered moments later.

"Stoops! That you?"

"Yup!"

"Your brother-in-law with you?"

"Yup!"

"Put your gun belts on your saddle horns -- then come ahead."

We did as instructed, unbuckling our pistol belts and refastening them so they could hang from our saddles. Then we continued leading our mounts toward the ranch.

A man with a Winchester in his hand came out of the main house and cradled the rifle in his arms as he made his way over to the corral and opened the gate. As we approached, I could see the man, Stoops identified as Dillman Chenowith. He looked to be a little older than Stoops but tough and used to working outdoors with his hands. He was short and wore a denim shirt and pants with well-worn but still very serviceable boots and a Montana peak, wide brimmed hat.

"Dillman," Stoops said as we walked our mounts into the corral.

"Stoops," he acknowledged. "Yank your saddle but leave the guns where they are."

We hung our saddles over the top fence rail.

"We've come a piece," Stoops said. "We need to rub'em down and get them some feed."

"Go ahead. Feeds inside that door," he pointed his rifle toward a side door into the barn.

When we were done, Chenowith nodded toward the ranch house and we all walked across and went inside.

An attractive young woman in her twenties served coffee as we sat down around the ranch mess table.

"What did you do with the Clancy brothers?" Chenowith asked as we drank.

"Liberty," Stoops told him.

"What's happened to you, Stoops? You used to be one of us?"

"Times are changing, Dillman. It won't be long b'fore the law comes in here and cleans house from top to bottom."

"And you figure to be the first?"

"All we're lookin' for is Amos Haggard."

"Yeah, we heard. 'Thought Haggard worked for you."

"He did. Then quit. Tried to frame my daughter's husband for a killin' he done."

"Heard that, too."

"Did you hear he shot Micah when he broke out of prison?"

"But he missed, they say. Only shot him in the leg. Haggard was never all that good with a gun from the saddle."

"You know where he is?"

"Nope, can't say I do."

"Can't or won't," I said joining the conversation for the first time.

"Haggard didn't kill your brother," Chenowith said to me.

"He was part of it. He stole the money from the bank hold up and somehow Ty Ayres got it in his head that Micah dug it up. We figure it has to be Haggard."

"Doesn't make him the killer of your brother and that's why you're here ain't it?"

"Haggard killed the bank clerk. Killed him when there was no reason."

"Nobody knows that."

"Anybody in the court room where they tried Micah because of Haggard's confession knows it," Stoops said.

Chenowith had no answer for this.

"Who are you?" Stoops asked the girl listening from the far end of the table, "Enid or Trudie?"

"Enid," she said.

"You're the older one."

"By eighteen months," she answered with a scornful look on what would have been a pretty face. "And I'm the tamer one.

"Trudie must be with Haggard," Stoops said.

"We didn't say that," Chenowith said somewhat surprised.

"You didn't have to. Everybody knows what your girls are like."

"And what's wrong with that?" Enid almost spat.

"Pretty only runs skin deep," Stoops said. "You two are known for what you do -- and who you do it with -- which is about damn near everybody."

Dillman reached for his rifle but I pulled Micah's revolver in the shoulder holster Stoops had given me. The rancher froze.

"Since you're not going to be much help to us," Stoops said, "we're goin'a trade horses and be on our way."

"If you mean horse stealing say horse stealing."

"We're stealing nothing," Stoops said. "The mounts we're leaving here are as good as anything you ever raised. I'm going to pick out a couple who are as close to being that good as you've got."

I reached across and took Chenowith's Winchester and levered it empty on floor.

"We'll leave this leanin' against a rock once we're out of sight," I said. "For now, both of you walk out ahead of us while Stoops does some horse tradin'."

CHAPTER 27

W e knew the Winchester I'd taken from Chenowith wasn't the only long gun on the place, but we didn't take time to look for any others. Stoops picked out the mounts we were trading for, then he took over watching both Dillman and his eldest daughter, Enid while I saddled up and put my gun belt back on. Stoops handed me the Winchester when he strapped his pistol back on.

We rode out in a trail of dust that would obscure us from anyone trying to back shoot us from the ranch. When we were clear and around the first turn on the trail, I parked the rifle against a boulder and we rode on.

Haggard and Trudie were at least two days ahead of us. We kept to the Outlaw Trail east out of Utah Territory and across the bottom of Colorado through the mountains. It was no easy ride and took daylight for us to make Durango. There we learned our quarry had bought supplies and spent the night before they left.

The next place they turned up was the coal town of Trinidad. They robbed a stage just out of town and killed the driver and a passenger, a preacher on his way to Denver. From there the trail turned south into New Mexico. The pair had been seen east of the Gallian River in a place called Las Vegas. They'd made a scene by coming into a saloon together where they drank and bullied anybody who gave them a disapproving look. They were loud and almost everyone in the bar left them to themselves. They found a room for the night and rode on the next day.

By sleeping on the trail, Stoops and I had made up some time. We were now about a day behind them. More than once the Deputy U.S. Marshal's badge had helped us trade for fresh horses. Stoops handled all of the selection of mounts. He had an eye for the best horse flesh and could spot flaws I'd never have noticed.

Down at the bottom of New Mexico the Outlaw Trail comes by Seven Rivers. There was only one river, the Pecos, but seven creeks flowed through the area into the river. Back in '78 this has been the headquarters for a group calling itself The Seven Rivers Gang during the Lincoln County Wars. It was on its way to being a ghost town when Stoops and I came through.

The few locals remembered Haggard and Trudie as a pair trying to raise hell in a place where there just wasn't much to be raised. They had ridden on after shooting out a few windows and scaring some children. They followed the trail southwest into Texas.

I had never been so far from Star Valley except when Micah and I had gone cowboying that one year. Stoops said he'd never seen lands so distant from Wyoming. This was desert grass lands, flat and only slightly rolling. The Pecos River ran shallow and clear over sandstone and was our companion across seemingly endless miles of Texas prairie. Blue Bonnets were in full bloom and as we forded and reforded the river keeping to the trail, more greenery, bushes and trees appeared.

Always I watched for Haggard's horseshoe with a nick in it. It told me they were ahead of us and when the tracks freshened with each passing day, we knew we were gaining on them. We were just lucky that the pair never changed horses.

In a town called Risien, Trudie had gotten into a cat fight with a whore in the only saloon. She pulled a gun and killed the woman, and then Haggard killed a cowboy who tried to come to the dying soiled dove's aid. The whole town was riled up and ready for a lynching but no posse had been formed. When they saw the badge I now wore on my shirt, they followed us as we moved out in pursuit.

Over the next two days, the posse dwindled. No one had provisions and while Stoops and I shared what we had, the men's enthusiasm evaporated after a hundred miles.

In the next town we traded horses once more and continued on our way with supplies I bought while Stoops tended to the horses.

At a new town called Midway Station, 'cause it was a half way stop for the Texas and Pacific Railway between Fort Worth and El Paso, we met a Texas Ranger about thirty. He was on the trail of bank robbers from a place further south called Uvalde. The Ranger's name was Hobie Declark. He was tall, stout, clean shaven with heavy lidded eyes that missed nothing. There was a rose colored birth mark high on his left cheek.

"I've seen them," he told us. "Passed'em on the road early this mornin'. They'll be in San Saba t'night, I wager."

"Then we will be, too," I told him.

"Be careful," the Ranger said. "We only exchanged nods as we passed, but I could tell there is death about those two."

"We know," Stoops said. "He murdered a bank clerk in Utah Territory and a cowboy back up the trail in Risien who tried to help a whore the woman had just killed. Further back they killed a preacher on a stage as well as the driver. We know who they are very well."

"'Wish I could go with you," he said. "But I get the feeling you two can handle yourselves."

"That's why we are the ones who came," I said.

CHAPTER 28

Our horses were lathered as we came into the town of San Saba. I saw a fresh imprint of the chipped horse shoe from Haggard's mount. We knew they were here.

We started walking our horses forward and saw an attractive young woman standing at a hitching rail in front of the bank holding the bridles of two horses, one of them Haggard's.

"She doesn't know us; so let's take it easy," I told Stoops. "Take your Henry and stop off at the general store. Keep everyone inside and tell them to get down."

"What are you going to do?"

"See that saloon sideways across the street and down from the bank? I'm going to pull in there and be ready for them."

Stoops nodded and turned off at the store. He had his rifle in his hand as he stepped inside while I moved on toward the saloon.

I got a quick glance at Trudie Chenowith. She wore a riding skirt, boots, and a solid blue blouse buttoned all the way up to her throat. Her hair was dirty blonde and hung to her shoulders. She was a beauty, no question. What a waste of God's gifts, I thought. I also noticed she had a Winchester lying flat on the hitching rail with her hand on the trigger.

Standing between the horses I put the Deputy Marshal's badge on the front of my vest. I had both my .44 Schofield and Micah's twelve shot .36 in my hands when a lean cowboy stepped out of the bar.

"Get back inside!" I said quietly but leaving no doubt in my tone. "Tell everyone to get away from the windows and the doors!"

Wide eyed and with his mouth wide open the cowboy backed up.

I ducked under the hitching rail and stepped up on the boardwalk but stood mostly behind a porch post.

Haggard stepped out of the bank with his .45 Colt in his hand, loaded saddle bags over his left shoulder. Trudie took the rifle and climbed into the saddle. Haggard turned back to the bank and raised his pistol to fire.

"Haggard!" I yelled.

They both turned toward me and Haggard fired taking a chunk of wood out of the post beside me. Trudie's shot missed completely but broke a window in the saloon somewhere back of me.

I fired at Haggard and he stumbled grabbing the rail.

Trudie levered another round into her rifle.

That was when Stoops stepped out and shot Haggard in the hip.

Trudie turned her gun on Stoops and fired. He grabbed the side of his head and fell back.

I shot with Micah's pistol and added a shot from my .44. She fell from the saddle.

Haggard managed to level his pistol in my direction, and I put two more slugs into him before he dropped to the boardwalk and rolled into the street face down.

I approached the pair with both of my pistols cocked. Trudie was on her back and her rifle a few feet away. Haggard still had his pistol in hand, his saddle bags spilling greenbacks and coins into the dirt. Neither one of them moved.

"Stoops!" I called over my shoulder to the store keeping my pistols ready as I poked Haggard with the toe of my boot. He was dead. So was Trudie.

"Damnit!" Stoops said stepping out of the store his handkerchief held to the side of his head. "She shot me in the ear. I'm bleeding like a stuck sow -- but I'll be all right."

From down the street a hairy, beer bellied man hurried up carrying a double barrel .12 gage and wearing a sheriff's star on his faded shirt. He cocked the shotgun as he approached.

People from the bank began to step out as did customers from the general store and men from the saloon.

"What the hell is going on," the sheriff asked stepping up to Trudie's body.

I put my pistols away and Stoops arrived to the site of the shootings.

"We were robbed," someone from the bank crowd called!

Another said, "I think the man was about to shoot one of us."

The sheriff kept his shotgun leveled in my direction. "Who shot the woman?"

"I did," I said. "Twice."

"She was holding their horses," Stoops said as blood ran down his neck and soaked his shirt.

"And the man?"

"Both of us," I said cocking my head toward Stoops.

"And who shot you?" the sheriff said to Stoops.

"The woman." Stoops said.

The sheriff lowered his shotgun.

"Who are you and who were they?"

"He is Amos Haggard. Escaped from Sugar House, Utah Territorial Prison. We know of five men he's killed, including a bank teller in a robbery over a year ago and a cowboy in a saloon a couple of days back. The cowboy was killed in Texas."

"The woman?"

"The daughter of a man who runs a ranch on the Outlaw Trail. Her name is Trudie Chenowith. They paired up awhile back. We've been on their trail from Wyoming to Utah Territory, across Colorado, down thru New Mexico and across Texas to here. Together they robbed a bank in Colorado -- and she killed a woman in New Mexico."

The sheriff stepped up and read my badge.

"I'm Russell Shepherd, sheriff of San Saba County," he said offering me his hand.

I shook it and said, "Joshua Guymon. My partner's Stoops Cowen."

"Mr. Cowen," the sheriff said with a tip of his hat. "Looks like we need to get you a doctor."

"And a stiff drink," Stoops said.

"Doc Palmer will have both. Somebody give the man a hand."

A couple of citizens stepped forward and helped Stoops off up the street.

I looked down at Haggard and Trudie. I felt bad about shooting a woman but I felt nothing for Haggard. And as I looked down on the pair, I found the ache for Micah hadn't diminished at all.

CHAPTER 29

D oc Palmer stopped the bleeding and patched up Stoops' ear.
"You've got to take it easy with this," he said as he worked
on Stoops. "Ears bleed a lot and if you break this open on the trail
somewhere, you could be in real trouble."

He was a man in his late 40's, bony with deep set, haunted eyes.
The sheriff had told me he was a good physician having earned his
skills during the Civil War. Almost twenty years later what he had
seen and done still defined his life.

We got him to eat with us that evening in the hotel dining room. I
told him about Star Valley and how peaceful life was up there.

"Sounds like a wonderful place," the doctor said. "But I think I'm
needed more here than I would be up there. I expect my main job
there would be delivering babies."

"True enough," I admitted.

"How soon can we ride?" Stoops asked.

"If you don't have any problems tonight, tomorrow would be
good. But go easy -- take your time. Make a few extra stops, maybe
even take a nap in the heat of the day."

"We'll do it, Doc," I said.

That night I wrote Emma a letter and mailed it at the train station before Stoops and I started out.

We did as Doctor Palmer said and it took us almost a month to get back to Cheyenne. We were leading the horses Trudie and Haggard had been riding. On the afternoon of the day we arrived at the Cowen ranch on the Green River, I asked Stoops, "Whose been running your ranch while we were away?"

"I'll be damned," he said removing his hat and scratching his head as we moved along. "I never once thought about it. I'll be lucky if the whole thing ain't burned to the ground."

Everything looked normal when we pulled in.

"At least it's still standin'," Stoops said. "And somebody painted th' barn."

We looked around and all the horses in the coral looked well fed and exercised. We climbed down and walked our mounts to the barn. There we unsaddled and rubbed down all our horses and saw to their feeding. After we cleaned up, we walked headed for the mess hall when Juanita met us on the steps where she had come out to ring the triangle.

"Señor Cowen," the cook beamed and rushed to take him in her arms. "You are back!" She stepped back and looked him over before adding, "And you are hurt." She lifted the hair over his still bandaged ear.

"Looks worse than it is, Juanita. How are things here?"

"Very good," she said.

"Who ran the place? I know we were a couple of hands short."

Putting her hands on her ample hips and pulling herself up to her full height, Juanita said, "I did. There was no one else."

"Well, looks t' me like you did a damn good job."

This brought a toothy grin to her face.

"But I have hired a new foreman."

"You have?" Stoops jerked upright. "Who?"

"His name is Armando Padilla. He rode in one day looking for work. Said he was looking for a job. He rode a beautiful caballo -- so I decided he must know something about horses. I put him to work. He showed me he was a hand and after two weeks I made him foreman. Running all of this was more than I could do without help. I hope he is good for you, señor."

"Juanita, if he's good enough for you, he'll please me like a fresh peach."

They laughed together.

A few minutes after Juanita rang for supper and we sat down, in walked the man I knew from before. He froze with his hat in his hand when he saw me sitting with Stoops.

"Señor Cowen," Juanita said noticing the sudden quiet, "this is Armando Padilla."

Stoops stood and offered the man his hand, "My new foreman, I hear," he said with a pleased smile. "Glad t' meet ya'. This here's my son-in-law...."

"Señor Guyman," Pedilla interrupted.

I offered Pedilla my hand.

"You two know each other?" Stoops asked.

"We crossed paths up the trail a while back," I said.

"Si," he said and shook my hand. "Señor Guymon gave me some good advice. I decided to take it."

"This is a great place for it," I said.

"All right let's eat," Stoops said and we all sat.

I reclaimed my gelding the next morning and Stoops took a fresh horse as we headed out in different directions. He was going straight up the western side of Wyoming to the valley and Geneva. I took Trudie and Haggard's horses with me as I crossed back west into Utah looking for Larn Duffy. I had a badge to return as well as the mounts that weren't mine.

It took me a couple of days to locate the Deputy Marshal. He was in Moab eating lunch in a cantina when I found him. His two companions were eating with him. I put the badge down on the table.

"You were right," I said. "It did come in handy."

Duffy didn't say anything for a moment. He just looked at the badge and back up at me.

"Did you get him?"

"Yep. And one of Dillman Chenowith's daughters. He'd brought out the worst in her. She killed a woman."

Duffy wiped his big mustache with the back of his hand and pushed out the one remaining chair at the table with his foot.

"Have a seat, Guymon."

I thought about it for a moment and decided to sit. Duffy signaled for another place and soon I had a glass and a meal in front of me.

"Stoops okay?"

"He got a chunk shot off one of his ears but he's fine."

"A gunfight?"

"They were trying to rob a bank. I think Haggard was about to kill someone in the bank after he stepped outside."

"Old habits don't change, I guess." This was his way of admitting he understood Micah was not guilty of the murder he was charged with. "You and Stoops were gone a while. Where did you catch up with them?"

"Texas. A place called San Saba."

Duffy shook his head and stuck out his lower lip indicating he'd never heard of it.

I took a bite of the beans as Duffy looked at his two partners. Without a word passing between them, the two took a last drink each, dropped money on the table, and left.

When we were alone he said to me, "You notice I've got a new badge?"

"I did. You're no longer a deputy. You're a full marshal."

"Of Utah and Idaho Territories. And empowered to appoint full time deputies as needed."

He hadn't reached for the badge I'd put on the table, yet.

"I'd like for you to keep that, Joshua," he finally said.

"I appreciate the offer -- but I don't think I'd pass the test."

"You already have. You've been cleared all the way up to Washington, D.C."

"Do they know I'm Mormon?"

"Might have forgotten to mention that. Like I told you, I don't believe in politics or politicians."

"Then how'd you get this new job?"

"Somebody moved up and they needed somebody for this job. I guess they knew I don't play favorites. The law's the law t' me. Same law for everybody."

I was so surprised I didn't know what to say.

"You know I live in Wyoming?" I said.

"Those are lines on a map. Most outlaws don't read maps or much of anything else -- but some like to see their picture on wanted posters. Utah, Idaho, Wyoming -- all the same."

I still hadn't moved.

"Joshua, there's good and there's bad. You know the difference."

I nodded my head.

"Raise your right hand," Duffy said. I did and he said, "That's it. Pick up the badge."

He shook my hand and I picked up the badge.

CHAPTER 30

Duffy and his two deputies wanted to go with me when I returned the horses to the Chenowith ranch.

Like I did with Stoops, I dismounted and walked in from about a half mile out. The others did the same. Duffy took charge of things stepping out in front of the rest of us. He was the one who hollered about a quarter mile away, "Hello, the house! Rider's comin' in!"

It was Enid who stepped out of the house with a rifle up to her shoulder. Like her younger sister, she was slender but filled out her long dress in the right places. Her hair was darker than Trudie's had been.

"I see your badges, lawman! What's your business?"

"Bringing back horses that belong to you!"

"We haven't lost any head!"

"Yes, you have, you just don't know it!"

"Stop right there!" she called.

We did.

"One of those is my sister's horse! How'd you come by it?"

"Put the rifle down and we'll talk!" Duffy said.

"I've have no reason to put it down! And I don't trust you!"

"We'll stay right where we are!"

118

She thought about this a moment and I called to her, "Your pa can keep us covered from the house!"

She looked back at the house then back to us. She started to lean the rifle against the fence.

"Shuck the shells, too!" Duffy yelled. "We don't trust you, either!"

She stopped with the rifle half way down and held it there.

"Do you want to know about your sister or not?"

She levered her Henry until it was empty and levered it twice more to show us it was clear. Leaning the rifle against one of the split rails she crossed her arms.

Duffy motioned to the half breed, Lute Quickdeer, who lead the two horses forward and slapped them on the rump starting them toward the ranch.

"Now speak!" she said.

"Haggard and Trudie are dead! They killed four people after they left here and were about to kill again in Texas!"

Enid reached for her rifle but Duffy's other deputy pulled out his rifle and sighted in on her.

"Don't!" Duffy called.

She stopped.

"You know what your sister was like -- and Haggard. They were like rabid dogs! They had to be put down!"

Enid was crying.

"If you want to know any more, come find me, Marshall Larn Duffy! They'll know where to find me in Liberty."

The horses were inside the fence now and except for the deputy holding the rifle, we swung into the saddle. Lute pulled his rifle and the other deputy mounted up. We rode off quickly, Lute bringing up the rear.

I was a hero to everyone in the valley by the time Stoops had told the tale of our chase to anyone who would listen. The story got better and more exciting with each telling and, of course, Stoops became a bigger part of it than he really was. Not that I wanted to contradict him. I'd already come to believe anyone who tells a story more than once is some part of a liar.

Being able to hold Emma and little Ester in my arms once again was all that was important to me.

Geneva seems to have come to terms with the loss of Micah, and she was now closer to her father, Stoops, than she had been before we left. Still, Geneva wasn't ready to go back to the Cowen ranch and he understood.

Claudine had become more of a daughter to Mama than a second wife to Papa and the two women had grown very close. Claudine's children, Polly and little Paul, were growing like buffalo grass.

Bishop Douglas came to see me when he heard about my marshal's badge. I told him about my conversation with Marshal Duffy. I was expecting a rebuke but he put his hand on my shoulder and said, "If anyone can help build a bridge, I think it may be you, Joshua. The marshal is right about your being a good man and I think the two of you are both doing God's work -- even if he is a gentile. If Utah is going to be a state in the union, and I think we will -- then we will have to make peace with the government and hope we can find good people there to work with."

"That's kind of the way I was thinking, Bishop."

"This doesn't relieve you of your duties as sheriff here in the Valley nor as a Danite to our faith."

"No, sir," I said, "I never thought it did."

The bishop, who owned the saddlery, must have spent part of the next a few more days saying the same things to others who came into his shop. I noticed people how began to treat me just as before.

I couldn't get enough time alone with Emma and she felt the same -- we both made it our main focus outside of Ester. Geneva got to taking more care of the baby for us.

The day Stoops left we had a little talk. He was a changed man. He'd joined us in meeting on Sunday and I think he was starting to smile more just as Geneva was.

He took my hand and said, "Thank you, Joshua, for lettin' me ride with you."

"I didn't think I was going to be able to stop you."

"True. But you could have made it a lot harder. We both know nothing is any better about Micah -- still, this was somethin' that needed doin'. Haggard and Trudie might still be out there somewhere hurtin' and killin' people. They needed to be stopped."

"Agreed," I said.

"The Texas Rangers would have been able to track'em down -- in time. I'm glad we were there to do it quicker."

I nodded.

"What about you, now?" I asked.

"Me. It's back to the ranch and ....."

"You ever think about marrying again?"

"Me? Who'd have an ol' coot like me?"

I let him think about that for a moment before I said, "Juanita."

"Juanita?" It was a thought he'd never imagined. His eyes darted back and forth for a moment before he said, "That's a lot of woman there. I wonder if she'd have me?"

"After the way she looked after your ranch, I'm thinkin' she just might."

This brought a real gleam to Stoops' eyes.

It seemed like he wanted to say more -- about something else -- but he couldn't find the words. After a few moments he sighed and climbed into his saddle.

Ester slept with Geneva the next couple of nights and left Emma and me alone.

I awoke one morning with the sun already up. I dressed and went to the kitchen where breakfast was on. There was also an open Bible on the end of the table, but I didn't pay any attention to it. I put my arms around Emma until she told me to sit down and eat.

Ester had gone with Geneva to gather eggs so we were alone. We didn't need to talk because we had said so much to each other in every other way the night before. But I had to tell her something.

"Don't you be surprised if there's another wedding in our family before too long."

She turned around and looked deep into my eyes.

"You've been thinking about it, too?"

"Have you've already discussed this with Stoops?" I asked.

"No," she said. "What about Stoops?"

"You haven't met her, but his cook, Juanita might be a good match for him. He's going to be lonely without Geneva there."

"That's not what I was thinking," Emma said as she went to the Bible and read to me out loud.

"Genesis 38:8 -- 'And Judah said unto Onan, "Go in unto thy brother's wife, and marry her, and raise up seed to thy brother."' She turned to another marked passage. "And Deuteronomy 25.5, 'If brothers are living together and one of them dies without a son, his widow must not marry outside the family. Her husband's brother shall take her and marry her and fulfill the duty of a brother-in-law to her.'"

Emma looked up at me.

"You know my mother was my father's third wife. You have a duty, Joshua."

"Stoops wanted to say something to me before he left -- but he couldn't get the words out."

"Then he might be thinking the same thing."

"Geneva isn't. It's too early. She still needs time. Maybe in about a year."

She came and sat in my lap. "Joshua, after last night, we may have another baby around here," she said with a twinkle.

"That's my duty," I smiled. Then more seriously I said, "Geneva is a pretty woman. She could find someone else."

"And if she doesn't?"

"We can talk to her about this if and when she's ready. In fact, maybe she should be the one to bring it up." Another thought occurred to me, "You haven't talked to her about this have you?"

"Only you, my love. I knew you'd never say anything about it, even to me, unless I said something first."

"All right. First things first. My other duties start here."

She stood up and said, "Your duty now is to get outside and take care of this place."

"That's not what I had in mind."

"Oh, I know. But we have plenty of time for other duties tonight."

THE END

TO GET TWO FREE E-NOVELS
BY
JACK R. STANLEY

ChroniclesMURDER IN MULESHOE
There's a killer in town. Do we hunt the S.O.B. down or throw him a
parade?

GUNS ALONG THE RIO
Two fresh-off-the-ranch 17-year-olds join the Texas Rangers in 1858.
What could possibly go wrong?

CLICK HERE

ABOUT THE AUTHOR

Jack R. Stanley is an award winning novelist, playwright, and screen-writer. As an officer and combat photographer in Vietnam he earned the Bronze Star. Yet he says, "When you're in a firefight and every-body else on both side have guns while you have a camera --- you get to change your pants a lot."

After his military service he received both his M.A. and his Ph.D. at the University of Michigan in Ann Arbor in Radio-TV-Film. His doctoral dissertation was on the long running TV series GUNSMOKE. Stanley also received two of Michigan¹s most presti-gious creative writing awards, The Hopwood Award, one for a one-act play and the second for a novel.

Still married to his gifted high school sweetheart, Stanley's first academic position was TV Area Head at The University of Texas at Austin's Department of Radio-TV-Film. He later moved to deep-south Texas and the Lower Rio Grande Valley for a challenging posi-tion with The University of Texas-Pan American. Here he taught Theatre-TV-Film for 30 years in the Department of Communication serving as Department Chair at U.T.P.A. for 11 years. He did take one year out to work for The University of Alaska Anchorage as a visiting professor. Back in Texas, Stanley directed for stage at The University Theatre, produced and directed fifteen student staffed, cast, and crewed feature films, writing most of the original screenplays. Just a few of his credits are available on IMDB.com.

He now lives in the Texas Panhandle where he writes his fiction and runs his blog, *www.TheFictionWritersNotebook.com*. His webpage is http://www.jackrstanley.com.

ALSO BY JACK R. STANLEY

Novels

[Political Fiction]

The Reluctant President

The Reluctant Incumbent

[Mysteries]

Murder In Muleshoe

Corpse In Canyon

The Lovecraft Murders

[Vietnam]

Through A Lens Darkly: Vietnam

[Westerns]

Guns Along The Rio

West Of The Frio

A Hard Line Between The Rios

The Mormon Marshal

The Gavel and the Gun

Short Stories

TALES FROM THE ALASKAN GOLD RUSH

Klondike Justice

Dangerous Camp On The Kenai

The Winds of Skagway

Screenplays

6 and 10

The 7th Luger

Afternoon Delight

Angel's Revenge

Between Love And Murder

Blood Drive

Death Scene

The Defection of Grigori Dorsky

The Evil Eye

Fatty and Hearst

Gideon: The Horse That Saved Texas

Hell In Paradise

Hollowpoint

Holiday For An Assassin

Horse Thief Hollow

Incident AtLajatis

Love, Lust, & Life

Mom & Apple Pye

Pancho's Pilot

The Prometheus Peril

The Rape of Sarah Quinn

Reservations

River of Tears

Seven Reasons Why

The Thing About Love

The Texas Rattlesnake Murders

Too Good To Be True

The Vampire Rose

A Violent End

The Virgin Casanova

Plays

www.ingramcontent.com/pod-product-compliance
Lightning Source LLC
Chambersburg PA
CBHW052000170626
46808CB00007B/2713